Milly Howard

The Case of the
SASSY PARROT

CRIMEBUSTERS INC.

2

JOURNEY FORTH™

Greenville, South Carolina

Library of Congress Cataloging-in-Publication Data
Howard, Milly.
   The case of the sassy parrot / by Milly Howard ; illustrations
by Bruce Day.
      p. cm. — (Crimebusters, Inc. ; Bk. 2)
   Summary: The young detectives of Crimebusters, Inc. investigate
a series of break-ins, with help from a back-talking parrot.
   ISBN 1-57924-721-0 (pbk. : alk. paper)
   [1. Parrots—Fiction. 2. Grandmothers—Fiction. 3. Mystery and
detective stories.] I. Day, Bruce, ill. II. Title. III. Series.
   PZ7.H83385 Cau 2002
   [Fic]—dc21

                                                  2002000930

The Case of the Sassy Parrot

Designed by Jamie Leong
Cover and illustrations by Bruce Day

©2002 Bob Jones University Press
Greenville, SC 29614

ISBN 1-57924-721-0

15 14 13 12 11 10 9 8 7 6 5 4 3 2 1

To the students in
Oakwood Christian School
in Anderson, South Carolina

Books by Milly Howard

Contents

Chapter One
A Call for Help

Boca Cay
Wednesday, January 17th, 4:45 P.M.

"Maria! Maria Delores!"

Maria Delores O'Donnell Ruiz looked up as the music in her ears abruptly disappeared. She removed her earplugs and pushed the CD tray back into her new CD player. "I didn't hear you, Mom," she said, turning down the volume. "You know, if you hit the pause button, the player won't pop open."

Her mother glanced at the lighted displays on the CD player. "I'm afraid I'll mess something up," she replied. "That thing has more buttons than Great Aunt Tia's wedding dress."

Maria grinned. Her mother had made it clear that she didn't share the family's love of technology. Her resistance when Uncle Luis wanted to modernize the house by wiring appliances electronically was the favorite topic of family gatherings. "What's the matter?"

"Your Gran is on the phone," Mrs. Ruiz replied. "She hurt her arm, and she wants to talk to you about Gasparilla."

Maria scrambled around and reached for the portable phone. The Gasparilla Festival in Tampa was second only to Christmas in her opinion, and she didn't want to miss a minute of it. Eagerly, she spoke into the receiver, "Gran?"

"Now, don't you worry, Maria Delores. It's just a sprain," Gran said. "But it is slowing me down. I really need help in getting our float ready for the parade next month. Could you come down on the weekends to help me out? Will that be okay? You and your friends?"

"Yes! Yes!" Maria replied, jumping around with the phone. *"Yes!"*

"Wait a minute! You don't have any projects due at school, do you?" Maria's mother frowned. "I forgot to ask you first."

Maria covered the receiver with her hand.

"There's a science fair coming up, but it's voluntary. I'd rather help Gran. I'll have all my schoolwork done before the weekends." She held her breath waiting for the answer.

"Well, it's settled then," Mrs. Ruiz said. "I don't mind driving you down. I'll be able to check on Gran's arm without annoying her. She's *so* independent!"

"Just like the rest of us," Maria said, laughing.

Mrs. Ruiz smiled and pushed Maria's curly hair back from her eyes. "Just like you anyway."

She took the receiver from Maria and settled down for a chat. Maria Delores grabbed her jacket from the hall closet and headed for the door. "I'm going to ask the others," she called back. Her mother waved absently, and Maria closed the door.

The Crimebusters' Headquarters
Wednesday, January 17th, 5:15 P.M.

Outside, she loped down the street toward Mark Conley's house. Skipping the house, she headed for the garage, taking the outside steps two at a time. She pounded on the door under the sign that read *Crimebusters, Inc., Private Investigators.* A small note had been added to the side. *For Hire.*

Adventures in the sleepy seaside town of Boca Cay weren't a dime a dozen. The action had been slow since school started. *With nothing else to do, Mark will want to help,* Maria Delores thought. *Corey too.*

When no one came to the door, she pushed it open. "Hey, anybody here?"

"Come on in, Maria Delores," Mark answered without looking up. He was hunched over a computer set up on an old, battered desk.

"It goes here, Corey," he told the boy beside him.

Corey pushed a cable connector into the modem port on the back of the computer.

"Way to go!" Mark said. He clicked an icon on the computer and a series of telephone noises crackled in the air.

"You're connecting!" Maria exclaimed. She leaned over Mark's shoulder. "How . . . Where . . ."

"Late Christmas present," Mark said happily. "Dad set up the account for us."

"But how are you going to pay for the service?"

"Chores," Mark replied. "And from what we earn from the Crimebusters. THIS will get things moving along."

Eyebrows raised, Maria looked at Corey.

Corey's braces glinted as he grinned at her. "Might," he said in answer to her silent question.

He pulled a chair up beside Mark and pushed his glasses back up on his nose. *Well,* Maria thought, *why not?*

"Great," she said out loud as a triple row of buttons appeared on the screen. *More buttons than Great Aunt Tia's wedding dress* flashed through her mind. She grinned and suggested, "Try Sports. Uncle Ramon said Alligator Jack's doing an online interview today."

"Alligator Jack? Wow!"

The next hour dissolved in a flurry of facts and faces. Maria Delores didn't look at her watch until her stomach rumbled. "Time to go," she announced. "Suppertime."

As she turned to leave, she remembered why she had come over. "Hey, guys," she said, raising her voice to get their attention. "Listen up."

Mark's hand reluctantly paused on the mouse. "What?"

Maria filled them in on the details of her grandmother's problem. "What about it? Want to go with me?"

She knew how much Mark and Corey had enjoyed the Gasparilla Festival weekend they had spent at her grandmother's house in Tampa. Their answers caught her by surprise.

"We can't," Mark replied. "We're working on a project for the science fair. Right, Corey?"

Corey nodded, absently tugging at his short hair. "I'm sorry, Maria Delores. I'd like to help, but we got this thing approved and now . . ."

"Okay, okay," Maria said. "I'm not pushing you or anything."

Mark took off his Atlanta Braves cap and sat back in the chair, concern on his face. "Will we leave you shorthanded?"

"I don't think so," Maria Delores replied. "The workers in the shop help, of course. But it won't be the same without you guys."

"If we finish early, we'll come along," Mark promised.

"Okay." Maria sighed and reached for the rope that hung from a loft rafter. "I'll take the back way out," she said. "See you. If you change your mind, let me know."

Chapter Two
Trouble

Boca Cay Marketplace
Thursday, January 18th, 4:15 P.M.

"I just have to pick up some snacks for you and Julio to take with you," Mrs. Ruiz said as she parked the van. She and Maria walked to the doors. "I'm so glad you agreed to take Julio with you. Since the boys usually go, Julio has been sort of left out, don't you think?"

Maria Delores groaned silently. The last thing she had wanted was to look after her seven-year-old cousin, Julio. "We don't mean to leave him out," she said. "It's just that he's such a baby."

Mrs. Ruiz looked surprised. "He's only two years younger than you are, Maria Delores."

"Mom, I'm ten!"

"Well, three years then. That's not so much."

"He's always into things, Mom."

"Not on purpose, I'm sure," her mother replied, smiling at Maria Delores. "Remember, he's independent . . ."

"Like the rest of us," Maria Delores finished, managing a smile in return.

The doors of the store swished open. Travis Burke stepped through, holding a bag of groceries. Maria Delores's first thought was that his jacket was too little. Her second thought was that his arms and legs seemed to have grown three inches over the holidays.

"Hi, Maria Delores. Ma'am," he said.

"Why, Travis. How are you doing?" Mrs. Ruiz beamed at the blond haired boy. "Are you shopping for your aunt?"

"Sort of," Travis replied. "We ran out of stuff."

Maria Delores peeked in the bag. "Stuff? Chips and cookies and candy," she said. "Rot your teeth."

Travis bared his teeth at her. Very white, even teeth, Maria Delores noticed. She heard the word Gasparilla and her attention snapped back to the conversation.

"Right," Travis was saying. "It's great. I usually go the day school lets out for the festival." His eyes brightened even more. "I know all about Gasparilla. And other pirates too. Did you know that Jean Lafitte was called the Gentleman Pirate? He turned down thirty thousand dollars and a Royal Navy commission, choosing instead to fight for the United States. Without Lafitte, Andrew Jackson might not have won the battle of New Orleans."

"I'm impressed," Mrs. Ruiz responded with interest. "Maria Delores is going down on weekends to help her grandmother prepare a float for the children's parade. Maria, Travis looks like he would be a good, strong helper. What do you think?"

"He's probably busy like the others," Maria Delores said, looking at Travis. "They're doing a science project."

Travis shifted the bag in his arms. "I'm not."

Maria Delores's heart sank. "You're not?"

She hadn't left Travis out on purpose. She just hadn't even thought of asking him. Technically he wasn't one of the Crimebusters—only an associate.

Now she was surprised at the resistance she felt toward including him.

But Travis looked at her strangely, and she suddenly found herself stuttering with embarrassment. It wasn't a feeling she liked.

"M-Mom . . ."

"Well, Travis, ask your aunt if she can spare you for a few weekends," Mrs. Ruiz smiled warmly. "I'm sure Gran would love to have you."

Travis shifted his gaze from Maria to her mother. "Thank you, Mrs. Ruiz. I'll let you know today."

Maria watched glumly as he headed across the parking lot toward a station wagon. *Well, I'll bet I know what that answer will be,* she thought. *Mark and Corey are one thing. Julio and Travis are another. Now I'm stuck with a trouble magnet and a "big brother"!*

Mrs. Ruiz looked at Maria curiously. "Why *didn't* you ask Travis?" She stepped aside as the automatic doors swished open, letting Maria enter first. "I thought he helped solve your mystery last summer."

"I honestly forgot," Maria Delores replied. "But . . ."

"But what?"

"He treats me like a kid," Maria Delores burst out.

Her mother's eyes widened in what Maria Delores called her wise woman look. "Like you treat Julio?"

"That's not the same," Maria Delores protested.

"Isn't it?" Mrs. Ruiz smiled gently and headed toward the produce section. "Why don't you give it some thought?"

"Yes, Mom." Maria Delores sighed and followed her mother.

"Promise?"

"I promise."

Chapter Three
Back in Action

Tampa Bay
Saturday, January 20th, 4:15 A.M.

Maria Delores opened her eyes and stared into darkness. She turned in the bed and reached for her alarm clock. Her groping fingers found nothing but empty space. Then she touched the carving on the bedside table and remembered that she was in her grandmother's house.

A scraping noise brought her upright. Heart pounding, she stared at the dark shadow at the foot of the bed.

"Maria? Did I wake you?"

Maria Delores let her breath out in a shaky gasp. "Mom! What are doing?"

"I'm getting an early start back, and I didn't want to wake you," her mother said, whispering. "We got here so late, I thought you kids could use the extra sleep."

Maria switched on the lamp. "I'm awake. Can I help?"

Her mother leaned over to kiss her. "Just go back to sleep. Take care of Gran for me, okay?"

"Okay, Mom." As Maria switched off the light, she heard a door open and close downstairs. You'd have to get up pretty early to beat Gran, she thought drowsily.

Gran's House
Saturday, January 20th, 6:17 A.M.

The next thing she heard was Julio's voice. "Wake up, Maria Delores! Wake up!"

She opened one eye and groaned. Julio hiked up his pajamas as he trotted from her bed to the door and back in a frenzy of impatience. "Come *on,* Maria Delores. Come and see the parrot!"

"Parrot?" Maria Delores yawned and turned over, clutching her pillow. She wasn't surprised that there was a parrot in the house. A parrot was nothing compared to the time she had been licked awake by a lion cub. Since Gran owned a pet store not far from her home, her house often became a temporary home for animals that were sick or just not adjusting to the shop.

"Maria Delores!" Julio jumped on the bed and bounced hard, dark eyes sparkling behind his glasses.

"All right," she said as Julio tugged at her. "I'm coming!"

She pulled on a robe and followed him downstairs. Julio ran across the tiled floor and disappeared into the dining room. Maria Delores stopped abruptly in the arched doorway. Travis was dressed and sitting awkwardly at the Mission Oak dining table, poking at something in a bowl. The thought of Gran's healthy, this-is-good-for-you meals, brought a rush of sympathy for unsuspecting Travis, but she squelched it when she remembered the trip down from Boca Cay. The two boys in the back seat had tried to outdo each other in insults. Far too many of them had been about girls. The memory made her frown.

A movement in the corner caught her attention, and she focused on the bird. It stopped preening its gray-green feathers. Turning its head to one side, it gave her a haughty look. "Awk! Look what the cat dragged in," it squawked. Then it hopped from its perch and waddled into the kitchen.

Travis grinned as Maria actually tried to straighten her sleep-tangled mass of curly hair, but Gran sighed. "He's a problem, Maria. He's so mouthy that I can't sell him. As a matter of fact, I can't even keep him in the shop. The other day he told one of my best customers that she walked like an elephant. I *think* he said walked. She *is* a big woman."

Julio giggled.

"It's not funny." Gran frowned. "I can't even send him back, because I didn't order him. He came in a shipment from South America. No one, and I mean no one, can account for him!"

A shriek came from the kitchen. A flour-spattered parrot shot into the dining room, claws clattering on the polished floor. He scooted to his perch and scrambled up, using his beak and claws to hoist himself up the pole.

"Inez?" Gran called. "Are you okay?"

Inez, Gran's cook, appeared from the kitchen. She shook a wooden spoon at the parrot. "You stay out of my kitchen or you'll be a piñata for mice," she threatened the parrot. She turned to Gran, "I thought Juan was standing behind me asking for pancakes, so clear he was. Makes my skin twitch!"

"Juan?" Maria Delores asked. "But your husband isn't here!"

"Tell *him*," Inez waved her spoon at the parrot. She started back through the open door.

The parrot turned his head to watch her leave. Then he fluttered down to Julio's shoulder. "Boy, one look at that cook'll scramble your eggs for good!" he said in Travis's voice.

Inez popped back around the door and gave Travis an indignant look.

"It was the bird!" Everyone spoke at once.

Inez shook her head in disgust and went back into the kitchen, muttering to herself.

"Whew!" Travis said. He looked at the bird. "How does he do it?"

"He imitates voices, any voices," Gran said with a sigh, rubbing her injured arm. "Some that you don't want to hear. I hoped that you children could re-train him for me."

Julio reluctantly put the parrot back on his perch and sat down at the table. "I can do it," he said confidently.

"I'm sure you can, Julio," replied Gran. She shook her head as he reached for a bowl. "Wash your hands first."

Maria Delores sat down on the empty chair beside Travis and glanced again at his untouched bowl. Remembering the bag of cookies and chips he had been carrying from the grocery store, she understood immediately why the creamy cereal in the bowl had only been stirred.

When Gran left the table to answer the phone, she whispered, "I forgot to tell you that Gran doesn't have anything in the house that isn't good for you. She believes in keeping in shape."

"No cookies? No cake?" Horror edged Travis's voice.

"It isn't so bad," Maria Delores said encouragingly. "There's fruit and . . ."

She stopped as Gran walked back into the room, a worried frown back on her face. "What's the matter, Gran?"

"Nothing. Whoever it was hung up again. Or we're getting someone else's ring. I'll call it in today," Gran replied, massaging the fingers of her right hand. "At least it wasn't another break-in at the shop."

Maria Delores sat upright and Travis dropped his spoon. "Break-in? You didn't say anything about burglaries!"

"Third time in two weeks," Gran replied. "I didn't want to worry your mother. Nothing taken— just things scattered and thrown about pretty much like they did to Mr. Valdes' shop last month. It's probably vandals."

Maria Delores glanced at Travis. His eyes were bright with interest. "Maybe they were looking for something," he suggested.

"I don't know what it could be," Gran replied. "I don't keep money at the shop overnight, and there is nothing there except the animals."

"Sounds like a mystery to me," Maria Delores said, trying to sound cool and professional.

Travis didn't bother. "I could do a stakeout," he told Gran enthusiastically. "I'll catch your vandal!"

Gran blinked. "Why yes," she said. "I heard about your last adventure. The Crimebusters, wasn't it? Maybe you *can* help! You too, Maria."

Maria Delores and Travis looked at each other. She watched him stonily, eyes narrowed.

"Am I in or not?" she demanded, prepared to fight for her position on the team.

He nodded reluctantly. "In."

"Then the Crimebusters will take the case," she told her grandmother. "We're back in action!"

Chapter Four
Missing Jewels

Gran's House
Saturday, January 20th, 9:00 A.M.

"Me too," Julio said stubbornly.

"No way!" Maria Delores replied, shaking her head. "This is business. You'll just have to stay with Inez. She'll let you help make lunch."

Julio's bottom lip poked out as Maria Delores planted her hands on her hips. "But . . ."

Maria Delores didn't move. She had baby-sat Julio long enough to know that if she showed any sign of relenting, she had lost the battle.

This time she won. Julio shuffled down the hall to the kitchen, his thin shoulders hunched and his head drooping. Travis looked at him in alarm, but Maria Delores choked back a laugh. "He's good," she whispered. "Just watch."

The closer Julio got to the kitchen, the more he drooped. He hesitated at the arch. When they didn't call him back, he finally disappeared through the doorway. After a moment, Maria Delores silently motioned Travis to follow. They peered around the door. Julio was up on a stool beside Inez, stirring a sauce.

"See? Now let's go!" Maria Delores whispered. Travis grinned and followed her back down the hall. As they passed the dining room, they heard the parrot squawk, "Thief! Thief!"

Maria Delores and Travis froze. "Shh!" Maria Delores hissed angrily. "Troublemaker!"

The parrot turned to look at her and fluffed up his feathers. "Awk! Where'd you get that wig?"

"Wig? Wig? He did that on purpose," Maria Delores insisted as Travis pulled her into the foyer. "That's the rudest . . ."

"He's just a parrot," Travis replied impatiently. "He couldn't possibly have done it on purpose."

"I agree with Inez. He'll be a *collectible* parrot if he keeps that up," Maria Delores said, looking back at the parrot.

She bumped hard into Travis, who had stopped suddenly. He was staring at the painting that hung over the hall table. Maria Delores chuckled. "Pretty bad, isn't it?"

"Well . . ."

"Ever seen a black velvet painting before?"

Travis shook his head, moving closer. "It's cloth?"

"Yep," Maria Delores replied, inspecting the painting of what appeared to be a Spanish princess. "The last one was a bullfighter. This one is new. Look at the jewels she's wearing!"

"Are they real?" Travis asked, leaning over the table to touch the jeweled locket glued to the lady's throat.

"Of course not," Maria Delores said. She opened a drawer and took out a small notepad. Travis put it in his pocket. Maria frowned, but continued, "Gran gets the paintings from Mr. Valdes. You know, the other shop that was broken into? He loans her a new one every few months."

"Did he take the bullfighter back?" Travis asked as Maria Delores opened the door. "Can I see it?"

"Come on then," Maria Delores said, pleased that Travis was really including her. "That'll be our first stop."

La Paloma Courtyard, The Galleria
Saturday, January 20th, 9:11 a.m.

Outside, they turned left on a tree-lined street already laced with sun and shadows. One more left turn and they were on Market Street.

"This is neat," Travis said. "Your grandmother lives downtown."

"Well, in the older part of downtown," Maria Delores said, avoiding a planter and heading for a shop with a green striped awning. "Most of the regular stores moved out along the main streets, but this area still does good business. It's a popular place for tourists. They think it's quaint."

"Quaint?" Travis looked at the planters and benches under the trees that separated the sidewalk from the narrow street.

"Cute, I guess," Maria Delores said. "Mr. Carlton, who owns the pharmacy down there," she pointed toward the end of the street, "wanted to take out the trees so more people could use the sidewalk. It gets so busy on festival day that people walk in the street."

"Why didn't they?" Travis asked.

"The other shopowners voted him down. They like the area the way it is."

She pulled open the door of the Galleria. Bells chimed as she stepped on the mat on the wooden floor.

"Hi, Mr. Valdes," Maria Delores said to the small man emerging from the back of the store.

"Just unpack the crates," he called to someone behind him. Then he hurried toward them.

"Maria, Maria, Maria," he exclaimed, holding out both hands. "It's good to see you again. How is your grandmother's arm?"

"It'd mend faster if she would stay still," Maria Delores replied.

Mr. Valdes smiled. "Impossible. You know your grandmother. Always busy; always on the . . . how do you say . . . ah yes, move. Now who is this young gentleman?"

Maria Delores introduced Travis, who had found the bullfighter painting and was inspecting it with awe. "I hear someone broke into your shop too, Mr. Valdes," Maria Delores said. "What happened?"

Mr. Valdes threw up his hands. "Ay, people nowadays. Nothing is sacred. My paintings . . ."

"They didn't take any?" Maria Delores looked around at the brightly painted furniture and pottery from Mexico.

"Not the paintings, Maria. Just a few of the paste jewels. They cut some of the paintings up a little, but I have a local artist who repaired them for me. They're as good as new," Mr. Valdes replied. Then he hesitated and added, "Almost."

He motioned toward a group of paintings marked For Sale. Maria Delores and Travis moved toward them. They were all black velvet painted in bright colors. Maria Delores shook her head. "Imagine," she said, inspecting the glittering "jewels" glued to the fabric as necklaces, collars, and belts. "They're getting pretty fancy with these."

"A new artist," Mr. Valdes said proudly. "He's from Bôgotá and has a fine future here."

"Bôgotá?" Maria Delores reached for the notepad, but Travis moved away from her and took out a pencil. There was nothing she could do. Helplessly, Maria Delores watched him write down the date. She shook herself mentally and began asking questions. Mr. Valdes gave them the details of the robbery, which Travis wrote down carefully. As they left the store, Mr. Valdes asked, "Is your grandmother already back at work?"

"She's on her way," Maria Delores said before she closed the door. "Can't keep Gran down."

O'Donnell's Pet Shop
Saturday, January 20th, 10:00 A.M.

Down the street, Maria Delores and Travis stopped in front of the pet shop window. "Kittens!" Maria Delores exclaimed, watching them tumble about in strips of newspaper. "Look at this one!"

A thin, brown arm swooped down and a hand lifted the kitten closer. Maria Delores blinked, then looked up. "Julio!"

"How'd he get here?" Travis asked. "We left him in the kitchen."

When they went inside, they found Julio sitting on a counter sharing chips with the parrot. Travis focused on the bag of chips and forgot all about Julio. He licked his lips hungrily.

"How did you get here?" Maria Delores asked Julio sternly.

The parrot tried to speak but just scattered bits of chips in the air. Before Julio answered, he adjusted the bright scarf he was wearing as a cape. "Gran brought me," he said. "We're going to get a ruby."

"A ruby?"

"We need one to put back on the lady," Julio tried to explain, handing another chip to the parrot.

"Give me those," Maria Delores said in exasperation. She reached for the chips and handed the bag to Travis. "I don't think parrots are supposed to eat chips."

"They eat crackers, don't they?" Julio replied indignantly.

"Crackers aren't chips. Now what ruby?" she asked again.

"On the lady by the door," Julio replied patiently. "It's gone."

"But it can't be gone," Maria Delores said. "It was there when we left."

"Gone now," Julio said, sliding off the counter. The parrot, still sputtering, wobbled, then clung tightly to Julio's shoulder as he hurried to the back of the shop. He shouted, "Gran, I'm ready!"

Maria watched him go without comment. Thinking hard, she turned back to Travis. He was holding the bag as if *it* contained jewels. "He forgot the chips," he said hopefully.

"Oh. You can have them," Maria Delores said. "He won't mind."

"Sure?" Travis took out one chip and placed it in his mouth. "Mmmm."

Maria Delores grinned. "Junk food attack, huh?"

Travis nodded, reaching for another chip.

Maria returned to the thought that had been nagging at her mind. "You know, Travis," she said, "That ruby was on the necklace when we left. Someone took it right after we went out that door."

"But no one was there except your grandmother, Julio, and Inez," Travis mumbled through a mouthful of chips. "They're not likely suspects."

"You're right." Maria Delores stopped. "And that's what worries me. There must have been someone else in the house."

Travis stopped eating and stared at her.

"Who?"

Maria Delores frowned. "We can account for everyone this morning. That means . . ." She shivered. "There must have been a stranger in the house."

Chapter Five

Partners?

O'Donnell's Pet Shop
Saturday, January 20ᵗʰ, 10 A.M.

"An accident, vandals, a ringing phone, someone in the house, a missing stone . . ." Maria ticked off a list of the suspicious activities at her grandmother's house.

"Careful. You're beginning to rhyme," Travis said, a mocking glint in his eyes.

"Well, what do you think?" Maria Delores retorted. "And what about the parrot just showing up like that?"

"Maybe we should question the parrot," Travis suggested.

"Don't laugh," Maria Delores replied. "As soon as we are through here, that's just what I intend to do."

Travis followed her into the storeroom. "Girls!" he said under his breath.

Maria Delores stopped short and wheeled around. *"What did you say?"*

"Gerbils," Travis said hastily. "I said gerbils."

Maria Delores sniffed, not convinced. She was well aware that Travis thought girls couldn't hold their own in an investigation. *I'll prove him wrong this time,* she thought. *I'll borrow Julio's mini tape recorder. It will be a lot better than any old notepad—especially one I can't get my hands on.*

The float was out back in the covered alley. Half the streamers were already on the bottom, so it didn't take much effort to figure out what to do. Staplers and rolls of streamers in hand, the two went to work. They worked in silence for a while. Maria glanced at Travis from time to time, hoping he would make some effort to share his thoughts with her. Finally, she realized that any overtures would have to come from her.

"Remember just before we left?" Maria Delores asked, making another attempt to establish a partnership. "When the parrot yelled 'Thief! Thief!'"

"Uh," Travis grunted, driving a staple into wood.

"What if he really wasn't talking about us?"

"You mean he knew the person in the house?" Travis looked skeptical.

"He wouldn't have to know them. Just a glimpse of someone sneaking around might have him yelling insults," Maria suggested.

"Like he did at us?" Travis asked.

"Maybe it wasn't at us," Maria Delores said in exasperation.

"I don't know," Travis said. "Maybe he took the ruby himself."

"He? Who?"

"The parrot."

Maria Delores looked at him in disbelief.

Travis shrugged, once again impatient with her. "Well, parrots do like shiny things, right?"

"I think that's magpies," Maria Delores said, pushing the staple gun trigger a bit harder than she needed to.

This is not going to be easy, she thought. *Why was it so much simpler with Mark and Corey?*

"Let's stick to facts." Travis ignored her indignant look. "Number One. It has something to do with the jewels on those paintings."

No kidding, Maria Delores thought.

"Number Two. Two shops have been burglarized—the Galleria and the pet shop. Taken—nothing but paste jewels."

"The pet shop has no jewels," Maria Delores protested. "Maybe they took what they thought were jewels because there was no money."

"That'd make them kids then," Travis said. "No adult would think those were real."

"What about the one in the house?"

"That's my third point. Break-in at pet shop owner's house. Taken—a jewel, paste again. Maybe they had their facts wrong the first two times, or three times, as it may be."

"What facts?" Maria Delores frowned. "It just doesn't make sense."

"Then we're back to square one. It probably is just vandalism by kids."

"Maybe," Maria Delores said. "But somehow I just don't think so. Just in case, I'm going to keep an eye on that parrot."

And after lunch, that is just what she did—but not the way she had intended.

Gran's House
Saturday, January 20th, 1:14 P.M.

That afternoon Maria Delores cornered Julio in the hall. She wanted to borrow his tape recorder, but he was reluctant to hand it over.

"But Julio," she pleaded. "I just want to use it in the investigation. That's all."

"No way. I'm investigating too." He whipped a long scarf around his thin body. "I'm the one you never see; the one who sees all but is never seen, who . . ."

"Okay, okay, I get the point," Maria Delores said. "You can come along if you let me do the recording."

"Partners?"

Partners? The word echoed in her memory. She stared at Julio's eager face. *I'm treating him just like Travis treats me,* she thought. *Mom is right!*

She hesitated, then held out her hand. "Partners," she agreed.

"Okay." Julio pulled the recorder out of his pocket. "I get to take care of Kiwi though, don't I, Maria Delores?"

"Kiwi?"

"The parrot."

Travis stopped at the door. "How did you know his name?"

"I asked him," Julio said simply. He clattered down the stairs to the dining room. The other two followed.

"He looks like the outside of a kiwi fruit," Julio said. "Let's go, Kiwi."

The parrot hopped onto Julio's shoulder and ran his beak through the black hair over the boy's ear. "See, he likes me," Julio said. "I'm training him to be polite."

"Well, he hasn't said anything rude for the last ten minutes," Maria Delores said. "But won't he get away?"

"Can't," Julio said. "His wings are clipped."

On the way back to the store, Kiwi only caused one problem. When passing a woman with a baby in a stroller, Kiwi squawked in a perfect imitation of Julio, "Take it back!"

Julio quickly wrapped his scarf around Kiwi's head, plunging him into silence. He looked helplessly at the woman. The woman gripped the stroller handle and looked from one child to another, tight lipped.

"Sorry, ma'am," Travis said, clutching Julio firmly on the shoulder. "It won't happen again."

Maria Delores followed Travis as he hustled Julio along, trying not to laugh at her cousin's expression. The rest of the way, they kept the scarf wrapped around the struggling parrot. As they walked, Julio supplied them with an endless stream of facts about gray parrots, this one in particular. Finally Maria Delores interrupted, "How do you know all that?"

"Looked it up on the Internet," Julio said.

"Wha-at?! How?"

"On the computer in Gran's office," he replied. "You left me alone all morning, so Gran put me on the Net. I played three games of . . ."

"Gran has a modem." Maria Delores took a deep breath. "That means we can talk to Mark and Corey," she said. "They can help us solve this mystery."

"You, maybe. I don't need any help," Travis said. "I am going to ask Mr. Valdes a few more questions."

"What questions, *partner?*" Maria Delores asked, trying not to show her irritation.

"Oh yeah. Partner." Maria Delores didn't miss his guilty look. "For one," Travis continued, "I'd like to know where he was after we left this morning. He made a point of finding out where your grandmother was."

"He was just being nice," Maria Delores insisted.

"Nice? Like he's being nice to keep your Gran in paintings that seem to attract thieves? I'm going to get to the bottom of this right now." Travis turned and headed toward the Galleria.

The Galleria
Saturday, January 20th, 1:47 P.M.

Maria Delores and Julio followed Travis into the store. A young man was working at the counter. He looked up, and a thin smile barely lifted the corners of his mustache. "Ah, the kids," he said. "What can I do for you?"

"We'd like to see Mr. Valdes," Travis said firmly.

The young man turned back to his newspaper. Flipping a page, he said, "Try County Memorial. He's in Room 502."

"What happened?" Maria Delores asked, concern in her voice.

"He fell down the stairs. Near broke his neck," the man said. "Now off with you. I'm a busy man."

"We can see that, Mr. . . ." Travis let his voice trail off, waiting for a name.

"Keith," the man supplied without a smile.

"What are you doing here, Keith?" Travis asked.

"I'm the shop assistant," Keith replied, frowning. "What's it to you, kid?"

"How long have you been here?" Travis persisted.

Maria Delores, alarmed at Keith's expression, pulled at Travis's arm. Keith stepped around the counter. "Two weeks, Mr. Detective. Anybody on the street can tell you that. Now beat it!"

"Beat it!" the parrot repeated, imitating Keith perfectly. "Beat it!"

Keith relaxed. "Yeah. Listen to the bird. Out of here."

He followed them to the door. Outside they heard the click of a lock. Then the OPEN sign was flipped over. Big, bold letters announced that the store was closed.

"Closed at 10:15," Maria Delores said in wonder. "Gran said Mr. Valdes hated to close even for holidays."

"Well, he's closed now," Travis said thoughtfully. "What did you think of that?"

Chapter Six
Clues That Don't Add Up

O'Donnell's Pet Shop
Saturday, January 20th, 2:10 p.m.

"Do you know about Mr. Valdes, Gran?" Maria Delores asked. Through the office window she could see Travis and Julio at the cashier's counter. Travis was propped against the counter, totally absorbed in what the young cashier, Angel, was saying. Maria Delores couldn't hear them, but it wasn't hard to figure out what the conversation was about. All Gran's efforts to steer her teenage helper to natural foods had been totally ignored. Angel's oversized shoulder bag was a well-stocked snack bar. Travis had a blissful look on his face as he peeled back the wrapping on a piece of chocolate.

"Yes, I heard about his accident," Gran said. She ran her fingers through her gray hair, rumpling her neat curls. "I'll run over to see him tonight."

"Could we go too?" Maria Delores asked.

Gran looked surprised. "I didn't think you remembered Ramon that well, Maria. Of course you can go."

Maria Delores opened her mouth to tell Gran than she wanted to question Mr. Valdes, then shut it. *No wonder Mom's always telling me to think before I speak,* she thought.

Travis appeared in the doorway, licking his fingers. "Ready to work?"

"Coming," Maria Delores replied. She cast a longing look at the computer on her grandmother's desk, wishing that she had asked for Mark's e-mail address before she had left home.

Two hours later, the float had a thick fringe of streamers drifting in the breeze off the bay. Maria Delores shivered, hugging her thin shoulders. "It wasn't cold while we were working," she said. "But now I want my windbreaker."

"I'll get it," Julio said from the doorway. He and Kiwi had spent the two hours alternating between working on the float and helping feed the animals in the shop. Maria Delores looked up, intending to thank him, and froze. Twenty pounds of snake looped around Julio's thin shoulders. When the python stretched out to test the air in front of Maria Delores, she suddenly found something to do on the other side of the float.

"Cool, Julio," Travis said, admiring the snake. "He could make a quick meal of you—not to mention Kiwi."

"He's been fed." Julio launched into a description of the python's feeding habits. "He won't eat again for two months."

Travis let him run on for a few minutes before asking, "Where *is* Kiwi?"

Julio stared at Travis blankly. "I don't know."

"Are you sure you fed that snake? Kiwi was on your shoulder about thirty minutes ago." Maria Delores spoke from across the float, eyeing the snake cautiously. "Obviously he isn't now."

"I think I put him on the perch. I'll go see."

Mario Delores followed as Julio entered the store and started to ease the snake back into its cage. From the perch came a scratchy, uneven version of "A horse is a horse of course of course, unless that horse is the famous Mr. Ed!"

"Oh, how sweet," said a young woman. "Listen, Jamie, the parrot can sing!"

A toddler stepped in front of Kiwi, holding a plastic dinosaur in his left hand. The other hand reached out and clutched a red tail feather.

A muffled squawk from the perch was followed by a shrill shriek. Kiwi shot straight up into the air. The boy backed away, holding the tail feather behind his back.

"Thief! Robber!" shrieked Kiwi.

Julio dropped the snake and banged his head on the cage. Maria Delores ran after Kiwi, who was flailing wildly around the store, slamming into cages. The monkey's cage door swung open with the monkey hanging onto it. He leaped off the door, landing on Angel.

"911!" shrieked Kiwi. "Call 911!"

Angel pried the monkey off her head and tried to put it back into the cage. The monkey wrapped his arms and legs around the door so it couldn't be closed. Angel gave up and let him hang on the swinging door. As she hurried to the woman, he dropped to a row of cages on the floor, knocking them over.

Iguanas slid slowly into the aisle and lizards leaped across a table. The customer gasped and reached for her son.

"Jamie, come on!" She grabbed his hand and half pulled, half shoved him out the door.

"Close the door! Close the door!" Angel called to her as she struggled over the fallen cages.

She made it to the door just ahead of one of the bigger iguanas. "Okay. Okay," she announced to the others, hopping quickly over the iguana. "I shut the door. I don't pick up big, crawly things."

"Don't worry, Angel," Julio said, tugging on the iguana's tail. "I got him."

Maria Delores and Travis helped gather up the rest of the iguanas and lizards. "All accounted for—except for the monkey," Maria Delores said. She glanced out the window and saw the panicked mother trying to pry the frightened monkey from the boy's back.

"Oh, my," Gran said. She hurried across the street and retrieved the monkey. "I'm so sorry. Are you all right?"

"If that monkey scratched Jamie . . ." the mother began angrily.

"He didn't hurt me, Mommy," Jamie insisted. "Can I have him? I want the monkey, Mommy."

"No!" His mother shuddered. "We just came for goldfish. No monkeys! Definitely NO monkeys!"

Jamie began to cry. He rubbed his eye with the hand that still clutched the feather.

"What is that? Jamie, get rid of that dirty feather!"

"I'll take it," Gran said, her face set in a pleasant expression. "Let me help you."

When they were settled in the car, she closed the car door firmly. "Do come back when everything is settled. There'll be a gift certificate for Jamie when you return."

When the mother's irritated look faded, Gran added, "For goldfish, of course."

When she returned to the shop, Gran looked around at the now straightened store and the quiet children. Her gaze settled on the parrot, who was preening his remaining tail feathers.

He tipped his head and saw the tail feather. "Thief!"

Gran just looked at him. He met her gaze with a fierce look of his own. "Pip-squeak. Squatty toad," he squawked, "Thief!"

She and Kiwi continued to stare at one another. "Well," she finally said. "If someone plucked one of my tail feathers, I might have done the same thing. I don't really know. But not in my store! Maria Delores," Gran said. "Do you think your mother has room for a bird cage in the trunk of her car?"

"You want me to keep Kiwi?" Maria Delores asked.

"Do I ever," replied Gran fervently.

Chapter Seven
Enter a Stranger

County Memorial, Tampa Bay
Saturday, January 20th, 6:00 P.M.

"Let me keep Kiwi in my room, Maria Delores," Julio begged. "I'll take good care of him, I promise."

"Are you sure?" Maria Delores said. "He can be a lot of trouble."

"I like him," Julio replied. "And he likes me. See?"

He held out his arm. Kiwi leaped from his perch and inched his way up Julio's arm to his shoulder.

"Okay," Maria Delores agreed. "But you'll have to keep him on the perch."

"No problem," Julio said happily. He disappeared into his room with the parrot.

"Ten minutes," Gran called from downstairs.

Travis opened his door and came out into the hall, shutting the door quickly. Maria Delores looked him over. Longsleeved black t-shirt, black sweatpants, black Nikes.

She grinned. "Julio's cape is around here somewhere. Don't you want to borrow it?"

Travis gave her a puzzled look.

"Batman," she explained, waving a hand toward his outfit. Her dark eyebrows winged upward as his cheeks turned red. "Travis?"

"Forget it," Travis said bruskly. "I've got my reasons."

Uh, huh, Maria thought. *I'll bet you do.* And it looked like another solo operation. *Partner* was a word that evidently refused to stick in Travis's mind.

But even Batman had a partner, Maria Delores thought, *and you've got one too, Travis. Whether you know it or not.*

At County Memorial, they waited in the lobby as Gran talked to the receptionist at the counter. In a few moments, Gran turned and motioned for them to come with her. They met at the elevator.

"Ramon is in pretty serious condition," Gran said. "They finally said I could see him for a few minutes, but you kids have to wait outside. There's a seating area down the hall from his room. You can wait there."

Maria Delores saw the same disappointment on Travis's face that she knew was on hers. He tucked the notepad into a pocket of his windbreaker. Maria Delores released the minirecorder that she had been clutching in her own pocket.

They were all quiet in the elevator. Maria Delores glanced at Gran, who was lost in her own thoughts. It took three stops before she realized that Julio had punched every button on the elevator. He was standing by the panel, swinging a small drawstringed bag.

Maria Delores had opened her mouth to scold him when the doors swished open again. A tall man stepped in and reached over to punch a button.

"I don't think you have to do that," Maria Delores said sheepishly.

He glanced at her in surprise, then looked at Julio, who was now digging in the small bag. He grinned and nodded. Then he leaned back against the wall of the elevator and closed his eyes.

"Jet lag," he murmured.

"Oh," said Maria Delores, not wanting to intrude.

The elevator remained quiet until the doors swished open again. They all walked out the doors and headed toward the nurses' station.

"Ma'am," the man said, stepping courteously aside to allow Gran to speak to the nurse.

"Thank you, sir," Gran responded. Then, turning to the nurse, she asked to see Mr. Valdes.

The nurse moved from behind the counter. "This way, Mrs. O'Donnell. You have five minutes, no more."

"I understand," her grandmother said as they turned the corner.

As she, Travis, and Julio headed for the seats near a window, Maria Delores overheard the young man introduce himself as Antonio Valdes. "I would like to see my uncle, Ramon Valdes," he said.

"I'm so sorry, Mr. Valdes," the nurse replied, a bit flustered. "We can tell Mrs. O'Donnell that you are here. I'm sure she . . ."

"No, don't," Antonio said calmly, holding up his hand. "She will only be a few minutes, after all. I'll wait here with the children."

The nurse returned to her station. Maria Delores watched as Antonio Valdes approached them, a friendly smile on his face. Travis pulled out his notepad, and Maria Delores made a few mental notes about the man's appearance. Sunstreaked brown hair, just a bit too long, bright blue eyes. She looked again. *Yes, blue. Small scar over right eyebrow. Makes him look rather adventurous, as does the long trench coat. Love the trench coat.* She snapped on the recorder in her pocket. *Trial run,* she thought.

He stopped in front of Travis and held out his hand. "I'm Antonio Valdes. You came to see my Uncle Ramon?"

"Yes," Travis replied. "He owns the store down from Maria's grandmother's pet shop. We're sort of worried about him."

"And we are . . ." Antonio stopped and looked at the other two.

Travis hastily introduced himself, Maria Delores, and Julio.

"We are working on a float for the festival," Maria Delores said. "But we keep running into trouble."

"Trouble?" Antonio settled into the chair across from them and leaned forward, a friendly smile on his face. "What kind of trouble?"

"Oh, just a few break-ins," Travis said, talking man to man.

Maria Delores noticed that he was trying to downplay the mystery angle.

The man's right eyebrow rose, emphasizing the scar which showed white against his tan.

"Burglaries?" The man sounded concerned. "Uncle Ramon mentioned something about a burglary, but I couldn't get much out of him. He just insisted that I wasn't to worry."

Julio quit swinging his bag long enough to look at Antonio. "You don't look like Mr. Valdes," he said. "He's Spanish."

The man laughed, showing even, white teeth. "I look more like my mother, who was English," he said. "My parents died in a car accident in the Andes mountains."

"Oh, I'm sorry . . ." Maria Delores began.

"Don't be," he replied. "I was just a kid. Uncle Ramon more or less raised me."

Maria Delores couldn't help thinking of Travis's parents, who had also died in a car accident. She glanced at Travis, who looked away. "That's tough," she said.

"I got along okay by myself," Antonio said bluntly.

Maria Delores looked back at Antonio. He added smoothly, "With Uncle Ramon's help, of course."

"Here comes Gran," Julio exclaimed. He leaped out of his chair, dropping his bag.

Antonio reached over and scooped it up. He shook it, smiling. "What's this? Marbles?"

Julio shook his head. "Jewels," he said, holding his hand out for the bag.

"Gemstones," Maria Delores corrected.

"Right. Gran got them for me when she bought the ruby," Julio continued.

Antonio dropped the bag into Julio's hand. "That makes you one rich young man," he said, laughing. "I need a grandmother like that."

"Uh, huh," Julio said, hurrying away. "Come on, Gran. Kiwi is waiting on me."

Maria Delores stood up last. She was behind the others, so she was the only one who saw the young man stop short on his way to the nurses' station. He was looking at Julio, a puzzled expression on his face. When he focused on Maria Delores, the expression immediately disappeared, and he waved at her.

An impatient call from Julio got Maria Delores's attention and she raced for the elevator. On the way down, she remembered to click off the recorder.

Chapter Eight
On the Trail

Gran's House
Saturday, January 20th, 8:12 P.M.

Gran opened the back door. "Up to bed, kids. It's been a long day."

"Night, Gran," Maria Delores said, starting up the stairs. The two boys raced past her, scrambling to be the first one to the top. "King of the hill!"

"Boys!"

They stopped abruptly.

"Sorry, Gran," Julio leaned over the banister.

"Sorry, Mrs. O'Donnell," Travis added.

She flapped her hand at them. Walking into the living room, she touched the message button on the answering machine. As Maria Delores started up the stairs, the answering machine clicked on, then the sound of a phone hanging up followed. No message.

She shivered. Another mysterious caller.

Suddenly there was a scratching sound from the top of the stairs. The children stared upward. Travis crept toward the sound. Something crashed. Bits of broken glass landed on the top steps.

"Gran's porcelain vase," Maria Delores moaned. She followed the boys just in time to see Kiwi waddle into Julio's room.

"I thought you closed the door, Julio," Maria Delores said.

"I did! I did!" Julio was trying to pick up the broken pieces of glass.

Gran had heard the noise and was coming quickly up the stairs. "What happened?" she gasped.

"I think Kiwi broke your vase," Julio said. "I'm sorry, Gran. I *know* I closed the door."

"Don't worry about it, Julio," Gran said, picking up the larger pieces. "It wasn't expensive. I'll sweep it up. Go on to bed now."

Maria Delores followed Julio into his room just as Kiwi disappeared under the bed. Julio dropped the bag of stones on the bed and got down on his knees to coax Kiwi out. The bag slid to the floor and the stones bounced and scattered over the carpet. Maria Delores scooped them up, pulling a red one from under the bed. She put Julio's stones back in his bag; he put Kiwi on his perch.

"I know I shut the door," Julio said tearfully. "I was afraid Kiwi would get loose, so I was careful."

"Maybe you did," Maria Delores said thoughtfully. "We'll check it out in the morning."

That night, Maria Delores couldn't sleep. Unanswered questions kept spinning in her mind. She pounded her pillow into a crumpled mass, but still couldn't get comfortable. She was sitting up for the third time when she heard a creak.

Fourth step, too far to the right, she thought immediately. Coming up or going down? She listened over the beating of her heart. Again she heard a squeak. Tenth step. Going down.

She flung off her blankets and raced to the door. She was just in time to see a figure in black open the front door and step outside, closing it silently. *No you don't,* partner, she thought. *Not without me.*

Maria Delores ran quietly down the stairs and opened the hall closet. She grabbed a raincoat and a pair of old slippers from the hall closet. Then she opened the door and slipped out.

Travis had stopped to pull a black knitted cap over his blond hair. Immediately he became one shadow among many. Maria Delores strained her eyes to follow his progress along the tree-lined street. Once he looked back, but Maria Delores dodged behind a bush. Gran's raincoat was dark and covered her completely. The slippers on her feet made no noise as she closed the distance between them.

Travis ran across the brick street and disappeared into the courtyard. Maria Delores had no doubt about where he was headed. Following, she saw a flashlight beam momentarily pick out the gold letters of the Galleria. Then it danced down the alley beside the building.

Maria Delores forgot to breathe for a moment. Travis was headed for trouble!

La Paloma Courtyard
Saturday, January 20th, 10:00 P.M.

Maria Delores waited until Travis wriggled through the basement window that had been jimmied in the last break-in. When the flashlight glowed through the dirty glass, she opened the window and peered through.

Maria Delores was the best gymnast in her class. The drop meant no more to her than it had to Travis, probably less. Unfortunately, the shoulder flap of the raincoat caught on the broken latch. Her easy leap bungee-jumped five inches from the floor, jarring her teeth and straining her arms. She stretched her feet as far as possible, but touched only empty space.

She was hanging there, concealed by crates and boxes, when the overhead light flashed on. Maria Delores couldn't see Travis, just as he and the newcomer couldn't see her. She could only listen.

"Well, well," drawled a familiar voice. "Trying a little night crawling, son?"

There was a scuffle as if Travis tried to run and was caught. Maria Delores strained to hear.

"Let me go!" Travis demanded. "You can't get away with this anyway!"

"Get away with what?" demanded Keith. "Aren't you the one breaking in here? Did you do the last job too?"

"Me? No way," Travis exclaimed.

"Well, you're in my way," Keith snarled. "Just what I need—some kid messing up the night's work."

Maria Delores heard the sound of dragging and scuffling. Then a door slammed. "That ought to take care of you for a while," Keith said, breathing heavily.

She stretched again and felt the raincoat slip.

"Now how did . . ." Keith started across the basement. "I thought Valdes fixed that window."

Frantically she squirmed in the raincoat, trying to unbutton the front. Her full weight straining against the buttons made that impossible, so she loosened the belt and let herself slither downward inside the coat. She gave a sigh of relief as her feet touched the floor. She had no choice but to leave the raincoat hanging and head for the cover of the boxes.

As she started across the room, she heard a bump from upstairs. Keith heard it too. He stopped and turned toward the stairs again, moving quietly. Maria Delores peeked over the boxes. Her eyes widened. Although his back was to her, his shadow thrown across the basement wall clearly showed the object in his hand. A gun!

The shop assistant flipped off the light and opened the door cautiously. He moved catlike into the hallway. Then the door shut, and Maria Delores was left in total darkness. Moving carefully, hands outstretched, she picked her way around boxes, crates, and stacks of furniture. At any moment she expected something to crash to the floor, bringing Keith back downstairs.

She was halfway across the room when she stepped on something. She caught the edge of a carton to keep herself from falling. She felt along the floor for the object. The minute she touched its rubbery surface, she knew what it was. "The flashlight!"

With a sigh of relief, she switched it on. She moved the beam around the basement and found the only door below the stairs. Hurrying to it, she saw that it was fastened with an outside bolt. Gently she released and opened the door.

She yelped as Travis charged at her, a board held over his head. "Travis!" she hissed, shielding her head with her arms. "It's me!"

She ducked, and he managed to stop his lunge just in time. He dropped the board and whispered, "How did you . . . ?"

"Travis," Maria Delores stared at his eyes, the only part of his face not covered with charcoal. "What on earth?"

Travis didn't reply. He helped her unsnag the raincoat and stack boxes and crates to climb out the window. Taking the flashlight from her, he held the beam on a crate so she could see where to put her feet. Looking down, she saw part of a painting of a gray bird and paused, surprised.

Travis gave her a heave. "Hurry!"

She forgot about the painting and sprang upward. In a few minutes they were in the alley with the flashlight and the raincoat.

"Come on," Travis whispered.

At the corner of the building, car lights swept along the street. They ducked behind the trash cans and waited. A man came out of the shop, locked the door, and entered the car.

No overhead lights came on. The figures in the car remained hidden behind the brightness of the headlights. Then the car moved silently down the street and disappeared in a red glow of brake lights.

"Did you see who it was?" The whisper came from directly behind them just as a hand clutched Maria Delores's shoulder.

Maria Delores swung around, heart pounding. Travis was faster. His hands closed around the intruder's throat. A surprised shout ended in a squeak.

"It's Julio! Let him go!" Maria Delores said. As Travis released the boy, she held the light on him. "What are you doing here?"

"I'm backup," Julio said hoarsely, holding up a cell phone. "I saw you leave and thought you might need help."

Maria Delores looked at his beaming face and pushed back the words that threatened to spill from her throat. She swallowed and said quietly, "Good idea, Julio."

Julio beamed, and Maria Delores sighed. *Well, there's no turning back now,* she thought. Julio was in. She looked at Travis and found that he was looking at her, rather strangely at that.

"And you?" he asked.

"Me?"

"Why are *you* here?"

"I saw you leave and thought you might need help." She was puzzled at Travis's sudden grin until she realized that she sounded like Julio's echo.

"I guess partners have their good points," Travis said. "But . . ."

"Guys." Julio tugged on his arm. "Guys. *Guys!*"

A siren wailed in the distance. Travis looked down at Julio.

"Did you call 911?"

"No way," Julio said quickly, shaking his head. He put a hand to his shoulder. "Where's Kiwi?"

"You brought that parrot?" Maria Delores and Travis spoke at the same time.

"He wanted to come," Julio said, looking around worriedly. "Where is he?"

They started up the alley, shining the light in corners. "Kiwi! Kiwi!"

"We've got to get out of here," Travis said grimly as the sirens got closer. "Let's go, Julio!"

Maria Delores and Travis hustled a reluctant Julio around the corner. As they passed a phone booth, a deep voice froze them in their tracks.

"Halt! Who goes there?"

They turned around slowly, but no one was there. Julio let out his breath. "Kiwi?" he whispered.

Moonlight glimmered along gray feathers. Kiwi scrambled along the ledge above the phone book. Maria Delores followed Julio. "It is Kiwi," she said out loud. "The phone is hanging off the hook. You don't think . . ."

"*Absolutely* no way," Travis said from behind her. "Come on! Let's get out of here!"

Chapter Nine
Here Now; Gone Again

Gran's House
Sunday, January 21st, 7:00 A.M.

The next morning Maria Delores was the first one up. She hurried down the stairs and opened the door. Scooping up the paper, she went into the dining room. She spread it out on the table and flipped through the pages, looking for anything that might include last night's activities. When she found nothing at all, she sat down to enjoy the Sunday comics.

A creak on the stairs alerted her. She tiptoed into the hall and was leaning on the door frame when Travis came back in, empty-handed.

"Looking for this?" she said, holding up a section of the paper.

Travis frowned. "I thought I heard somebody."

"Not me," Maria Delores protested. "I know every squeaky spot on those stairs, and I didn't hit one of them."

"I guess that makes you the Queen of Sneak," Travis said rudely, reaching for the paper.

"Queen of Sneak, Queen of Sneak," his voice echoed from the top of the stairs.

They looked up to see Kiwi perched on Julio's shoulder. Hair standing in wild black shocks, glasses tilted on one ear, the thin boy regarded them with a frown.

"How am I supposed to re-train this parrot? Put earmuffs on him?" he said sternly.

Travis sighed. "Okay, Julio. I'm sorry, Maria Delores."

He raised his voice. "I'm sorry, Kiwi!"

"Sure," Maria Delores said, suddenly glad that she hadn't had time to respond to Travis's remark. As she put the comics down on the hall table, something in the painting above the table caught her attention.

She looked again. "Guys," she whispered tensely.

"What?" Travis was right beside her.

Julio headed down the stairs. "What's going on?"

Maria Delores pointed at the picture. "It's gone again!"

"What? What?"

"The ruby! It's gone again!"

"Maybe the glue didn't stick good," Julio said. He scooted under the table. Emerging emptyhanded, he shook his head. "Nope. Inez already cleaned."

Travis helped Julio up. "Is it in your bag?"

"No," Julio replied. "My bag's in my room."

"But I picked up a red one last night," Maria Delores said. "It has to be there."

"I didn't take it," Julio protested. "I don't have a red stone."

"Yes, you do," Maria Delores insisted. "I saw it."

They went to his room. He was still protesting when Travis picked up the bag. Travis handed it to Julio. "You open it."

Julio dumped the contents of the bag onto the carpet. "See?" he asked, looking up at them. "Just mine. No ruby."

When they didn't answer, he turned to look at the gemstones scattered on the carpet. Right in the center was a gleaming red stone. Julio blinked. "We put it on the lady. I helped glue it on!"

Maria Delores sat back on her heels and touched the stone. "Well, it's not there. It's here."

Travis held out his hand for the stone. "Hey, this doesn't look like the other stones. It's cut like a real jewel."

Julio settled his glasses on his nose and peered at the stone. "That's not the one Gran bought. How did it get here?"

Maria Delores took the stone back. "We'd better give this to Gran. She'll check it out for us."

They took it downstairs and gave it to Gran, who had just come in from jogging. She listened to their story as she examined the stone. "It looks like the stone that was originally on the painting. I don't know why it would be real. Some fakes are really good and can fool anyone other than a jeweler."

"Can we get a jeweler to look at it for us, Gran?" Maria Delores asked eagerly.

Gran nodded. "Why not? I'll give it to Mr. Danbridge at church today. He'll take care of it."

After breakfast, the children dressed for church. No t-shirts for today. Gran was a stickler for formality. Maria Delores had long since come to an agreement with both Gran and her mother. Frills and lace were fine as long as they were soft, not scratchy. As a result, Maria Delores was comfortable in her cream-colored dress. She beat her hair into submission with a stiff brush, wishing as usual that she had straight blonde hair like Melissa Crumpton. Sighing, she pinned it back and clipped it in a bow.

She wriggled her toes in her slippers as she inspected her image in the mirror. *I'll pass,* she thought. *Wonder how Travis is doing?* She grinned at the thought of Travis in a suit.

"Ready, kids?" Gran called from the hall. She adjusted her gloves as Maria Delores came down the stairs. "Nice," she said approvingly. "You too, Travis."

Maria turned to see Travis calmly descending the stairs in a neat navy suit. She blinked as he took Gran's arm at the door. "Let me help you down the step, ma'am," he said.

This is the Travis of the black shadows? This is the get-out-of-my-face Travis? Maria Delores was so stunned she almost shut the door on Julio and Kiwi.

"Uh, uh," she hissed. "Put that bird back."

"He wants to go," Julio insisted.

"Not to church," Maria Delores said firmly.

She waited until he returned. She locked the door and had Julio try it to make sure it was locked. Then they joined Gran and Travis at the car.

Maria Delores got in back with Julio. "I'm surprised he's not driving," she said under her breath.

Julio heard. "Can you drive, Travis?"

"Not likely," he replied. "Why?"

"Maria Delores wanted to know," Julio said cheerfully. "Ow!"

"Sorry," Maria Delores said. "My foot slipped."

Julio gave her an injured look, then turned back to the front seat. "Did you bring the jewel, Gran?"

"Yes, I did," Gran replied, watching traffic. "It's in my pocket. Don't worry. I won't lose it."

Grace Church, Tampa Bay
Sunday, January 21st, 11:00 A.M.

Gran's church had high-backed pews that gleamed with fresh polish, and the tall stained-glass windows made brightly-colored patches across the floor. And across people, Maria Delores remembered suddenly. After her first Sunday visit with Gran, she had gone home all excited about the colorful people. It had taken her mother a while to figure out what she was talking about.

A tall man standing by himself caught her attention.

"Mr. Valdes!" she exclaimed. "Gran, this is Antonio Valdes, Mr. Valdes' nephew. We met him at the hospital."

Antonio reached for Gran's hand. "So nice to meet a friend of my uncle's," he said warmly. "He has spoken of you often."

"He's better then?" Gran responded eagerly.

"Much better, but not enough to come home yet." Antonio smiled. "We must not rush his recovery."

"No, of course not." Gran moved down the aisle beside Antonio. As they continued to talk, she reached her usual pew and sat down, making room for Antonio.

The pews filled quickly, and Maria Delores looked around. She nodded at Mr. Carlton and his family. Looking past him, she caught her breath. A small, wiry man was making his way along the pew. He wore an old sweater and faded jeans. When she continued to stare, he fixed her with a hard look, then turned away.

"Look!" she hissed at Travis. "It's Keith!"

Travis groaned and slid down in his seat.

"Sit up," Maria Delores whispered. "He doesn't know it was you. You were covered with black, remember?"

"Oh, yeah." Travis sat back up.

Maria Delores frowned. "He's watching us."

Carefully Travis positioned himself so he could see Keith. After a moment he said, "No, he's not. He's watching Mr. Valdes."

"Antonio?" Maria Delores whispered back, a little louder than she had intended.

Antonio Valdes glanced at her inquiringly. Maria Delores smiled and lifted a hand in greeting. He nodded and went back to his conversation with Gran. Then the organ music swelled and the congregation stood. All conversation stopped.

As often as she could, Maria Delores glanced at Keith. The man's eyes were half closed. He appeared almost asleep. It could have been funny, but Maria Delores was sure he was not the slightest bit sleepy. There was something about the way he held his body that was watchful, waiting. Waiting for something in this pew. She shivered.

About twenty minutes into the sermon, Travis nudged her. "He's gone," he mouthed silently.

Startled, Maria Delores looked back. The seat Keith had occupied was empty. Travis and Maria Delores looked at each other uneasily.

"Get a drink of water?" Travis whispered, jerking his head toward the back.

Maria Delores shook her head. Whatever Keith was up to, Maria Delores thought, they could do nothing about it. Even Julio didn't try that thirsty bit on Gran. She turned her attention back to the sermon.

When they stood after the final song, Gran asked Antonio to have Sunday dinner at her house. He agreed, thanking her for being gracious to a visitor. He rode up front with Gran, and the children sat in the back. On the way, he talked about his life in South America. Maria Delores admired how he effortlessly included even Julio in the conversation.

Gran's House
Sunday, January 21st, 12:30 P.M.

When Gran unlocked the front door and opened it, sunlight made the bright colors of the painting glow. The empty spot where the jewel had been was as obvious as a missing tooth. Antonio stood looking at it as Gran put her car keys on the table.

She put his coat in the hall closet, and the children started up the stairs to put their own things away.

Maria Delores heard Gran apologizing for the flawed painting, explaining that the "jewel" was missing. Travis almost missed a step when he heard the next sentence.

"Do you mean this?" Antonio said.

"Oh!" Gran exclaimed. "Where did that come from?"

"It was on the floor next to the table leg," Antonio said.

All three children had stopped and were staring down into the foyer. Antonio held out his hand. Gran took the red stone carefully.

Maria Delores held her breath, waiting for Gran to pull out the other stone. Gran inspected the stone. She looked thoroughly rattled, but she didn't say anything about the one the children had given her.

"I'll just put this in the drawer for now," she said. "The glue must have come loose."

Maria Delores looked at Antonio. He was watching Gran strangely. When he answered, his voice was not quite as warm as usual. "I'm sure it did."

The children washed their hands in the hall bathroom.

"See," Julio said. "I didn't have it."

"Then what do you have?" Maria Delores said. "What's going on here? I thought you looked under the table."

"He could have missed it. But I still don't like it," Travis said. "Things just won't add up right. First we have a jewel. Then we don't. You buy a jewel and glue it on. Then it disappears. Then you do have a jewel. Then the other one reappears. Now we have two!"

A sudden squawk interrupted them.

"Kiwi," Julio said. "I'll get him."

"Gran won't want him in the dining room while we have company," Maria Delores warned.

"She won't care," Julio said, disappearing into his room.

Maria Delores shrugged. She and Travis went on downstairs. Gran sat her across from Antonio. When Julio appeared in the dining room door, Maria Delores was looking at their guest. The pleasant look disappeared, and a look of distaste darkened his face.

Kiwi's reaction was more dramatic. He flapped backwards, losing his balance and flopping to the floor. He scrambled toward the kitchen, squawking loudly in a voice the children had never heard. Spanish phrases rattled out so quickly that even Maria Delores only caught a word here and there. A few words of English mixed with the Spanish made it clear that the parrot was not being complimentary.

"Make sure Kiwi stays in the kitchen, Julio," said Gran firmly.

She turned to Antonio. "I'm sorry. Kiwi is extremely rude."

Antonio's expression eased into a pleasant smile. "Where did you get him?"

While Gran explained about the shipment, Maria Delores watched Antonio, but he seemed perfectly at ease. And he was quite a storyteller. She couldn't help but laugh at his suggestions on how Kiwi got to Tampa. She put her worries aside. Maybe he did find the stone on the floor. Julio probably missed it.

Travis and Julio seemed to have forgotten the stone already. Travis had found another fan of pirate lore. The boys chattered away with Antonio, filling the small room with tales of adventure and danger.

After lunch, Maria Delores helped Gran clear the table for Inez. "What did you do with the other stone?" She asked quickly.

"That's strange, isn't it?" Gran frowned slightly. "Two stones! I gave the first one to Mr. Danbridge. He said he would get back to me next week. Maybe then our mystery will be solved, Maria Delores!"

"I hope so," Maria Delores said. "This has been the most mysterious case ever!"

"It's just the second case," Travis said from the doorway. "Mrs. O'Donnell, Antonio said I could go back to the shop with him. Could I?"

"How about all three?" Antonio asked, towering over Travis. "Give you a little break in return for lunch?"

Gran smiled. "Maria's mom should be here in an hour or so. Maybe next trip down?"

"Sorry, buddy," Antonio said to Travis. "How about next Saturday? We'll order pizza and unpack some of those crates in the basement."

Maria Delores had no trouble reading Travis's expression. Searching through that basement was clearly something he wanted to do. She was thankful that Julio had caught Antonio's attention.

"Kiwi too?" Julio asked.

"Of course," Antonio said smoothly. "Bring the bird."

Chapter Ten
Trouble for Kiwi

Boca Cay

Sunday, January 21st, 4:30 P.M.

"You kids are certainly quiet," Mrs. Ruiz said as she eased the car up the ramp onto I-4. "What's going on?"

"Tired," Maria Delores answered.

"How's the float going?" Mrs. Ruiz asked.

Maria yawned. "Bottom's done. We'd have done more if it hadn't been for that parrot . . ."

"Kiwi!" Julio jerked upright. "Maria Delores, did you bring him?"

Maria clapped her hands to her mouth. "I forgot. Gran will be upset."

"No she won't," her mother replied, smiling. "She made sure that the parrot was caged and tucked into the trunk."

"Can he breathe back there?" Julio asked, twisting around as if he were trying to see into the trunk.

"Kidnappers keep people in trunks. Gagged, too," Travis said. "Sure, he can breathe."

Mrs. Ruiz laughed. "I understand Kiwi, as you call him, created quite a bit of trouble."

"Did she tell you we have a new case?" Maria Delores asked. "Crimebusters on the move! Yeah!"

She and Travis did a high five, or began one. Julio tried to turn it into a triple and got tangled up in their hands.

"Julio," Travis said solemnly. "You need someone to give you a few lessons. Like the master of cool here."

"Would you, Travis? Great!"

Maria Delores retreated to her book and tried to shut out the noise in the car. A combination squeal and shriek caused Mrs. Ruiz to push the brakes harder than she intended. "Boys!"

"It wasn't us," Julio protested. "That was Kiwi."

"No wonder Gran wanted you to take him home," she said, resuming speed. "Quiet down a bit and see if he'll settle down."

The rest of the trip passed in relative quiet. As they left the interstate and entered Boca Cay's city limits, Mrs. Ruiz slowed down to forty-five miles an hour. Ten minutes later, they stopped at Travis's house.

"See you in school, Travis," Maria Delores said sleepily.

"Sure," he replied, pulling out his duffle bag. "Uh, oh. Looks like I set off the alarm here."

"Close the trunk! Close the trunk!" Julio yelled, clapping his hands to his ears.

With the trunk dark again, Kiwi settled back down. Mrs. Ruiz groaned. "If tomorrow weren't a school day, I'd bring your bags over later, Julio. I don't look forward to opening that trunk again. Noisy, isn't he?"

Maria Delores stretched. "I'll take him out at Julio's."

"Can he stay with me, Maria Delores? Please?"

"Gran did tell me to keep him."

Mrs. Ruiz said quickly. "Oh, I think she just meant for him to be well cared for. Julio will do that, won't you, Julio?"

"Yes'm," Julio said solemnly, his glasses shining in the streetlight. "Kiwi and I get along fine."

With Julio and Kiwi safely inside, Maria Delores couldn't wait to get home to her own bed. A few blocks more, and they were home. Maria stumbled down the hall to her bedroom and fell across the bed.

"Maria Delores! Don't sleep in those clothes!" her mother called.

"Mmmm," Maria Delores replied.

Her mother came in, shaking her head. "You guys must have been up all hours of the night," she said, handing Maria Delores her pajamas. "Now, change."

When the bed was turned down, Maria Delores sank into it gratefully. She didn't even know when the lights went out.

Boca Cay Elementary
Monday, January 22nd, 10:00 A.M.

The next morning she made it to Mrs. Simon's fourth grade class just before the bell rang. Mark and Corey cornered her at recess.

"Give!" Mark said.

"Right," Corey agreed. "Where'd you get the parrot?"

"Kiwi? How'd you know about Kiwi?" Maria Delores asked, puzzled.

"Who doesn't know by now?" Mark grinned. "It's not every day that a parrot gets sent to the principal's office!"

Thoroughly confused, Maria Delores stared at her friends.

"Julio brought the parrot to school for show and tell," Corey said. "I guess it liked all the attention it was getting, because it . . ."

"His name is Kiwi," Maria Delores interrupted.

"Okay. Kiwi got carried away and said some things that Miss Jamison didn't like. And she couldn't get him to be quiet."

"Therefore," Mark said, grinning. "To the principal's office!"

"Is he still there?" Maria Delores was concerned.

"Nope. He got expelled." Mark's eyes sparkled with laughter. "Julio's mom came to pick him up. Now give!"

"Okay." Maria Delores took a deep breath. It took most of the recess time to fill the boys in on the strange happenings in Tampa. When she finished, the boys were wide-eyed with envy.

"Awesome!" Corey exclaimed.

"Crimebusters see action again!" Mark was delighted. "How's the investigation going?"

Maria Delores frowned. "Not too good."

"Not too bad." A voice drowned out what she was saying. Travis joined the group. "Hey, guys."

"So, what gives, Travis?" Mark asked eagerly. "What's going on?"

"Nothing much," Travis answered. "At least nothing you can put your finger on. Nothing adds up, but something's going down. We just can't figure out what."

The buzzer rang and students began heading for the doors. Mark said hurriedly, "Come over after school. Meet us in the loft."

Crimebusters Headquarters
Monday, January 22nd, 4:10 P.M.

So the first serious meeting since the *Case of the Dognapped Cat* began that afternoon. Just answering questions brought a lot of facts into the open. Soon the Crimebusters had several pages of notes.

Mark read them out loud, then shook his head. "I see what you mean, Travis. Lots here, but nothing adds up yet."

"Have you checked old newspapers?" Corey asked. "Sometimes that can give you a handle on what's happening around town."

"We're really there to work on the float," Maria Delores answered. "That doesn't give us much time to run around town."

"We can do it from here," Corey said.

"Here?" Travis asked.

"Here." Mark booted up the computer. "On the Net. There are several Tampa papers online."

"Right!" Maria Delores slapped her forehead. "I forgot!"

They gathered around Mark as he logged on. Then he brought up a search box and typed in *Tampa Tribune*. In a few minutes, the newspaper was on the screen. Narrowing his search to the few weeks before the weekend, he began to scan through articles.

"There!" Travis pointed to the screen. "That one!"

Mark brought up an article about recent burglaries in the Tampa Bay area. None of the break-ins mentioned bore any resemblance to the activities around Mrs. O'Donnell's neighborhood. Disappointed, they signed off.

"Checkmate," Maria Delores said with a sigh.

"Stalemate," Travis responded. "Not a clue."

"Maybe we should try some other things," Maria Delores suggested. "Like finding out about missing parrots or vandalism or something at least."

"We'll keep looking," Mark promised. "Just e-mail us, so we can keep up with what's going on."

Chapter Eleven
A Bold Pirate

Tampa Bay
Saturday, January 27th, 9:10 A.M.

The next weekend was sunny and warm. Mrs. Ruiz dropped the children off late Friday night and returned to Boca Cay. On Saturday morning, the eager children were out on the streets before Gran was ready to head to the shop. They wandered along the bay, breathing in the excitement that the pirate festival brought to town.

The morning breeze off Tampa Bay sent sun-sparkled wavelets rippling toward the embankments. Pirate flags flapped in front of the harbor stores, and bearded men with black eye patches roamed the streets promoting everything from appliances to a new French restaurant just off Biscayne Boulevard. Quite a few of the pirates were interested in Kiwi.

"Not stuffed, is he?" asked a red-bearded pirate packing two gun holsters and cowboy boots.

"No way, Yosemite Sam," said Kiwi in Julio's voice.

Julio laughed at the pirate's astounded look.

"What makes him think . . ." asked the pirate.

"It's how you're dressed," Maria Delores said. "I'm beginning to think this parrot watched way too much television."

"Me too," Travis agreed. "Or maybe his owner watched too much television."

The pirate inspected Kiwi, who scuttled closer to Julio's ear. "Want to sell him?" he asked.

Julio pushed his glasses up on his nose and stared at the man. "Kiwi's not for sale."

Kiwi turned a beady eye on the man and squawked. "No way, Sam!"

The man persisted until the children became uncomfortable. After again refusing to sell Kiwi, they walked on toward the pet shop. Maria said, "Travis, you may have a point about the television. But Kiwi couldn't turn on . . ."

"He can do most anything with that beak of his," Travis insisted. "I'll bet he could turn on a television."

"Sure could," Julio agreed proudly. "He turned on the gas stove at home. Mom just about had a fit. She said if we had not had a pilot light, he could have killed us!"

Maria Delores looked back. "Is that guy following us?" she asked indignantly. "No, no. Don't look back. It's the pirate who tried to buy Kiwi," she said. "Just keep moving. Julio, run on ahead with Kiwi."

Julio took off. The excited parrot squawked and went airborne, fluttering just over Julio's shoulder. Maria Delores and Travis stopped by the glass front of a furniture store and waited.

"What's he doing?" Travis hissed.

Maria Delores moved so she could see the pirate in a dresser mirror. "He's turning down Dempsey Street," she said quietly. "He's gone."

"He was probably headed that way anyhow," Travis said in disgust. "You're seeing play-shadows."

Maria Delores bristled. "I am not! It just makes sense to . . . wait a minute! Doesn't Dempsey cross St. Agnes?"

Travis looked exasperated. "How would I know? Why?"

" 'Cause I think it does . . . and Julio just headed for St. Agnes!"

Travis took off, long legs pumping as he ran. Maria Delores was right behind him, thankful for every soccer practice she had attended last fall. They charged around the corner of a brick building just in time to see the red-bearded pirate reach for Kiwi.

The alarmed parrot lurched out of reach, screeching different voices into the quiet morning air.

"911!"

"Reach for the skies, partner!"

"Car 54, where are you?"

As soon as he finished one imitation, he launched into another. He fluttered and wobbled around Julio, inches beyond the pirate's grasp.

Julio threw his light weight against the pirate's knees, trying to take him to the ground. Instead, the pirate held him off by placing a hand on his head. Julio flailed about furiously.

Kiwi struggled up on a shop awning and shouted in a woman's voice, "Don't shoot! *Ooooh, please* don't shoot!"

Curious people poured out of doorways along the street. They clapped as the pirate tried to climb up a post to reach the parrot. When Julio grabbed his ankle, the pirate shook his leg, trying to dislodge the boy. The first onlookers to reach them stopped laughing as the angry pirate dropped to the street and ran. By the time Maria Delores and Travis reached Julio and Kiwi, they were surrounded by a small crowd of puzzled people.

"I thought it was a street show for the pirate festival," a man said, helping Julio to his feet. "What's going on here?"

"He wanted the parrot," Maria gasped, trying to catch her breath.

"What people do nowadays," sighed an older woman. She clutched her purse tightly under her arm. "If they want something, they just try to take it!"

"Well, he didn't get Kiwi," Julio boasted. "Kiwi outwitted him!"

"Say, son," said Mr. Carlton, who had come out of his pharmacy. "Planned or not, that was quite a show. Your parrot could name his own price during the Gasparilla Festival. I'm not agreeing with thievery, but I can see the man's point. Kiwi's priceless as far as advertising goes!"

"Sure," came a sarcastic voice from the left. Maria Delores saw Keith lounging in the doorway of the Galleria. "Why don't we just put a perch up for him in the courtyard?"

Mr. Carlton replied eagerly, "Good idea! Say, kids, what about it?"

"Nope," Julio said. "Kiwi stays with me."

Chapter Twelve
Dark Shadow

O'Donnell's Pet Shop
Saturday, January 27ᵗʰ, 9:30 A.M.

Gran was working so intently on bookkeeping that Maria Delores decided not to bother her. She followed Travis and Julio to the storeroom.

Attaching the papier-mâché animals to the pet shop float was the part Maria Delores liked best. Angel had made the chicken wire frames and had molded the animals with help from her art class at school. As a result, the brightly painted animals had a decidedly Spanish attitude.

It took Maria Delores a few minutes to realize that the animals were caricatures of people they knew. "Look," she said, laughter in her voice. "The gorilla is Mr. Carlton, and the ostrich is Gran!"

"You're seeing things," Travis scoffed. "Mr. Carlton is thin, not big and muscled."

"Forget the bodies," Maria Delores insisted. "Look at the expressions. That's Gran—that upward tilt of her head when she is looking through her bifocals!"

"Maybe," Travis said reluctantly as he inspected the gorilla. Then he grinned and held up a kitten with tangled tissue fur. "Maria Delores?"

She giggled. "Okay. Now let's find you and Julio."

A young lion and a small monkey proved to have Travis's and Julio's expressions. Travis moved on to the snake. "And who's this?"

Maria Delores took a second look. The snake didn't look like anyone she knew. She shrugged. "Don't know," she replied. "Look, the parrot is Kiwi!"

Delighted with the lively-looking creations, they spent the morning arranging them on the almost finished float. Gran and Angel came out to look at the result.

"Best one ever," Gran said with pride. "Angel, you and the kids have done a great job. I just wish I could have helped more."

"Not to worry, Mrs. O'Donnell," Angel said cheerfully. "Doing the float is the best part of my job. You know, I've been thinking. Maybe we should paint a mural on the bricks outside the shop. A jaguar would be nice . . ."

"I'll have to think about that one," Gran interrupted hastily. "Why don't you sketch it out first?"

Angel pulled a pencil from her elaborate hairdo and tapped her long, crimson nails on the counter. "Maybe the Amazon . . ."

Maria Delores grinned. "Angel has style. Whatever she and her friends do will be great," she reminded her grandmother. "You always like it when it's done."

Gran took a deep breath, then smiled. "You're right. Now, Maria, weren't you supposed to meet Antonio for lunch?"

Maria Delores turned to look at her grandmother. "I almost forgot, Gran. Did you get a report on the red jewel?"

Gran shook her head. "Mr. Danbridge was in Europe this week. He said he would call me when he got back."

Disappointed, Maria Delores joined the others. "Detective work isn't easy," she complained.

"Maybe we're going at it wrong," Travis said, holding the door for her. "We've been busy, and this isn't Boca Cay. It's not that easy to pick out clues when you don't know what is normal and what isn't. We need to find out more about Keith. Maybe we can figure out what he's up to."

The Galleria
Saturday, January 27th, 11:47 A.M.

Julio tagged along behind them, feeding Kiwi peanut bits from a candy bar. Maria Delores glanced back once, then followed Travis into the quiet of the Galleria.

Antonio was in his office with a man. It wasn't Mr. Valdes. Maria Delores was positive that she had never seen this man before, yet he looked familiar. Antonio looked surprised to see them, then smiled. "Hi, kids," he called. "Be with you in a minute!"

He came out, shutting the door of the office. Curiously, Maria looked in the glass window. She saw the man's shadow. Then the blinds closed.

Behind them, the door chimed again as Julio pulled it open. Kiwi gave a muffled squawk and slammed backward into the closing door. Antonio frowned as the frightened bird flew awkwardly around the room. A pottery bowl crashed to the floor.

"Get him, Julio!" Maria Delores missed the bird by inches.

Julio cornered Kiwi in a triangle of paintings and captured him. Antonio shook his head. "I'm sorry, Julio, but the bird can do a lot of damage here. Why not put him in my office?"

Maria Delores reached for Kiwi. "I'll do it," she said quickly. Before Antonio could respond, she had reached the office door and opened it. She went inside, expecting to see the man. No one was in the office. Quickly looking around, she saw another door.

As she started forward, Kiwi squawked uneasily. Antonio spoke from the showroom door, startling both Maria Delores and the bird. "You can use the coat rack as a perch," he suggested.

Kiwi made a whimpering sound.

Maria Delores stroked his feathers. "You'll be all right here, Kiwi," she whispered, placing him on the coat rack. He hunched his head down into his feathers and refused to look at her. She left him reluctantly, still wondering who the man was and where he had gone.

Antonio had already returned to the counter with the boys. Travis and Julio were bent over a clear paperweight containing a large scorpion. "Wow," Julio said, adjusting his glasses. He turned the paperweight, magnifying the tail segments of the scorpion. "It's huge!"

"There's more on the shelf behind you," Antonio said. "Take a look at this one."

He handed Maria Delores a paperweight. She turned it gingerly, trying not to look at the enlarged fangs of a pygmy rattlesnake.

"Cool!" Travis said, reaching for a tarantula paperweight. "Where did you get these?"

"I made them myself," Antonio said. "It's a hobby of mine."

He took the paperweight from Travis and turned it gently in his hands. "There's a story behind every one." He smiled. "Maybe someday I'll tell you a few."

Maria Delores kicked Travis lightly. Keith had appeared at the top of the basement stairs, arms loaded with boxes. "Uh," Travis grunted. "Yeah. Can we help you with those boxes?"

Keith looked from them to Antonio. His face was unfriendly. He spoke rudely. "If I needed help, I'd ask for it."

Antonio smiled. "No need for rudeness, Keith. The children came to do some work this afternoon."

"Where?" Keith was blunt. "I don't want kids underfoot."

"There are some crates in the back corner that I want unpacked," Antonio's voice rose slightly.

Keith's expression didn't change, but his protests stopped. He stood aside to let Antonio lead the children down the stairs. At the foot of the steps, Maria Delores looked back to see Keith still holding the boxes. He met her eyes and scowled. The door slammed behind him as he went into the showroom.

The crates at the back were stacked haphazardly near the small window Maria Delores and Travis had climbed through. There were a lot more than Maria Delores had expected, and she sighed. This was not her idea of investigating, but evidently to the boys the boxes were treasure chests just waiting to be opened.

When Antonio handed Travis a crowbar and left them alone, Maria Delores wished she could wipe the smug expression off Travis's face. She knew what was coming next, and she was right.

"Step back, Maria Delores," he said. "These crates could splinter."

She moved aside and resigned herself to the role of observer. Watching Travis and Julio wrestle with the crates quickly became boring, so she turned her attention to the crates themselves. Stenciled on the sides was the name Gato.

"Look at this!" Travis exclaimed as he pried the top off.

"Bones!" Julio said happily, picking up what looked like the skull of an antelope.

Maria Delores stepped back. She didn't care for dead things. Moving around the stack, she read the names stenciled on the crates. Ciudad, Argentina, Peron, Bogôtá, Joaquin.

"Pizza's here," called Antonio from the basement door.

Travis dropped the crowbar and made it up the steps before the other two could respond. When they arrived, he was opening the first box of pizza.

"Help yourself," Antonio said. "There's plenty."

Maria Delores looked around. "Where's Keith?"

"He went to pick up a new shipment," Antonio replied. "Keith can be what you call a deadbeat . . . No, a dead . . ." He paused for a moment, searching for a word.

"Dead weight?" Travis supplied, grinning.

"Pretty gruff, isn't he?" Antonio looked amused. "But he's a good worker, and he shows up every day. I think he knows as much about this business as my uncle does."

"How is Mr. Valdes?" Maria Delores asked.

"Better. He'll be home tomorrow," Antonio replied. "Stop by. He'll be glad to see you."

Julio had just finished his third slice of pizza when they heard a thump from the office. "Kiwi!" Julio said. "He likes pizza too!"

He pulled the office door wide open. Maria Delores saw the shop assistant kneeling over something on the floor. She leaped to her feet and was right behind Julio when Keith moved, revealing a gray lump of feathers on the floor.

It was Kiwi!

Chapter Thirteen
Snake Man

The Galleria
Saturday, January 27th, 12:47 P.M.

Keith looked at the children. "I didn't do it," he exclaimed. "I came in and found him lying on the floor."

"Yeah, right," Travis said.

Maria Delores pushed past Keith and knelt beside Kiwi. Julio joined her.

"Is he dead?" He blinked, his eyes watery behind the lenses of his glasses.

Maria Delores picked up the limp body of the bird. "Not yet," she said. "Let's get him to Gran."

Travis held the door as Maria Delores carried Kiwi gingerly. Julio ran ahead, yelling for Gran. She came to the door of the pet shop, shading her eyes to see them as they hurried down the sidewalk.

"Kiwi's hurt!" Julio shrieked.

Gran turned back to the shop and called for Angel to bring her keys and purse. She met them at the car. It was a short trip to the vet, but it seemed like miles to Maria Delores.

Dr. Allen's Office
Saturday, January 7th, 1:10 P.M.

The vet was a short man with thin, wispy hair. His cheerful expression disappeared when he saw the limp form in Maria Delores's hands. He took Kiwi gently and disappeared into the clinic. The children sat restlessly on the hard seats. Gran filled out the necessary forms. Every time the doors swung open, they all looked up expectantly.

Finally the receptionist came out and talked quietly to Gran, looking at the children with sympathy. Maria Delores groaned.

Travis pulled out his notepad. "Who was in the room with Kiwi? Keith. Who . . ."

"I don't want to be a detective right now," Maria Delores said sadly. "I just don't."

Travis put the notepad away. "Right."

Gran came back to sit beside Maria Delores. "It looks like Kiwi was poisoned," she said, disbelief in her voice.

"Poisoned!"

"Who would do a thing like that?" Julio was close to tears again.

"Could he have eaten something that made him sick?" Maria Delores asked. "He was always snacking on something."

"Afraid not," Gran replied. "A small dose, but it didn't take much."

"Didn't?" Julio was standing by Gran's knees. He leaned on her. "Didn't?"

"To make him really ill," Gran explained quickly. "He is just a very sick bird."

"But he isn't dead?" Julio's voice wavered.

"Not y . . . No, he's not dead," Gran replied in a firmer voice. "We'll need to leave him in Dr. Allen's care."

"But . . ."

"Julio, Dr. Allen has taken care of my animals for a long time," Gran said softly. "He will do his best for Kiwi."

O'Donnell's Pet Shop
Saturday, January 27th, 3:48 P.M.

Back at the shop, the children were quiet. They sat outside on the steps near the float. Angel brought them drinks, then just shook her head and went back inside.

Travis was the first one to break the silence. "We can't just sit here and wait," he said impatiently. He got up and began to pace back and forth. "Think, Maria Delores! Kiwi was all right until we went into the Galleria."

"No," Julio said suddenly. "He didn't want to go in. He was acting funny."

"And we didn't pay any attention to him. We just shut him up in an old room while we . . ." Maria Delores stopped. "That man! If Keith is telling the truth, then the man we first saw must have done something to Kiwi."

"*If* he is telling the truth," Travis said. "But I guess we have to explore all the possibilities. Keith did look sort of funny when you picked up Kiwi."

"Funny?"

"Yeah. Like he was sorry or something." Travis shrugged. "What about the other man? He looked just like any other man."

"Except for one thing," Maria Delores said, remembering the look on the man's face. "I've seen him somewhere."

"On the street? In a shop? There are hundreds of places you could have seen him," Travis said, a little sharply.

Maria Delores turned away and sat looking at the float. A breeze caused the swing for the parrot to move. The parrot's tissue feathers ruffled slightly. Maria Delores glanced at him and looked away. To keep from thinking about Kiwi, she looked at the kitten, then at the lion. Her gaze dropped to the lion's paws. She was looking directly at the snake. Her breath caught in her throat. She jumped up, pointing at the snake.

"What? What?" Travis sound alarmed.

"Snake," Maria Delores said. "It's the man! That's where I saw him!"

Travis sat back down. "Then you don't know the 'mysterious' stranger. Somebody else probably saw him."

"Yes," Maria said, her eyes alight. "Somebody did. And Angel knows who!"

Travis was back on his feet, discouragement gone. "You're right! Great job, Maria Delores!"

Beaming, Maria Delores hurried after Travis. A bewildered Julio followed behind.

Angel threw up her hands in mock surrender as they surrounded her. "What's this?" she asked.

"Who did the snake?" Travis asked.

"I did," Angel replied in surprise. "You don't like the snake?"

"No, I mean, yes," Travis replied. "But who was the snake?"

Angel laughed. "You mean you saw that?"

"The animals look like people," Maria Delores said. "We know everybody except the snake. Who is he?"

"Most people never see anything except the animals," Angel said, frowning. "Hope I don't get into trouble over this."

"Not from us, you won't," Travis promised.

"It's the snake I'm worried about," Angel said. She tapped her long nails on the counter nervously.

"Who is he?" Maria Delores repeated.

"Monroe B. Thornton," Angel said, lowering her voice. "He's a successful realtor in town. Very successful. Very rich."

"There's no law against that," Travis said, disappointed.

"No," Angel continued. "It's where his money really comes from that makes him a snake. People say he's a thief, big time."

"What kind of thief?" Travis asked.

"Don't know. Different things, I guess. He almost got busted a couple of months ago, but his lawyers got him out of it somehow."

"How did you know that?" Maria Delores asked.

"Word on the street," Angel replied. "The man's bad news."

Maria Delores stared. "Bad news," she said thoughtfully. What was someone like that doing with Antonio? And how did Keith fit into the puzzle?

Chapter Fourteen
Missing

Gran's House
Saturday, January 27ᵗʰ, 4:13 P.M.

Gran took them back to the house. The rest of the afternoon seemed to drag on. Travis had disappeared.

"Probably off on his own again," Maria Delores muttered. So much for the budding partnership.

"Maria Delores." Julio's voice was forlorn.

She looked down at him. "What, Julio?"

"My bag's gone."

For a moment she didn't understand. Then she remembered the bag of stones. "What happened to it?"

"I had it in the Galleria," he replied. "But when Kiwi got sick, I guess I dropped it."

Maria Delores got to her feet, grateful for the action. "Go tell Inez that we're going back to the shop," she said. "We'll stop by and pick the bag up on the way."

But the Galleria was closed. Maria Delores stared at the Closed sign in the window. Julio didn't say anything.

"Come on," Maria Delores said. "We'll go to the pet shop."

O'Donnell's Pet Shop
Saturday, January 27th, 4:47 P.M.

Angel offered Julio a candy bar, but he just shook his head. He went over to the cages and stroked the python. Maria Delores gave them a wide berth and went outside to put some finishing touches on the float.

When she came back in, Gran was hurrying out the door. "Be right back, Maria Delores," she called. "You have e-mail from Mark Conley. I meant to tell you about it, but I forgot."

Maria Delores hurried into the office. She quickly located the message and opened it. *See what you think about this*, she read. *I couldn't find anything in the Tribune, so I widened my search.* Attached was an article from a Colombian newspaper. *ARTIST DIES IN ANDES MOUNTAINS*, she read in shock. She scanned the rest of the article, reading of the accident that took the life of Mauricio Herrera, a young artist from Bogôtá. The reporter wrote that the young man had recently made sales in the United States and had a promising future. The accident was still under investigation and might involve an international gang of jewel thieves.

Maria Delores caught her breath as she read the last paragraph. The young artist had a hobby. He trained birds. The picture with the article showed the young man with his favorite, a gray African parrot named Kiwi.

"Kiwi," Maria Delores breathed. Bogôtá. The young artist from Bogôtá who had a promising future. Bogôtá. Bogôtá.

The words clicked around in her mind. She shut her eyes and saw the crates in the Galleria. The stencils on the sides swam across her closed lids. Argentina, Colombia, Bogôtá. Young artist from Bogôtá. Jewels. Stolen jewels!

O'Donnell's Pet Shop
Saturday, January 27th, 5:07 P.M.

Maria Delores charged out of the office, startling Angel, who dropped her nail polish. "What is going on here?" Angel asked in exasperation. "First Travis, then Mrs. O'Donnell, then Julio, and now you! It's like everybody has gone crazy!"

"Where did Travis go?" Maria Delores asked.

"I don't know. Nobody tells me anything. Just 'back in a minute, Angel'," she complained.

"Well, where's Julio?"

"I don't know. He had that slithery snake wrapped around his neck. He just walked around and around. Then he was gone too," Angel answered. "So's the snake, which suits me fine. What is going on?"

"I wish I knew," Maria Delores said grimly. She headed for the door. She wasn't sure about Travis, but she had a good idea where Julio was. And she didn't like it one bit.

The Galleria
Saturday, January 27th, 5:10 P.M.

Outside, she looked down the street at the Galleria. The late afternoon sun glanced off the windows, making it impossible to see in. Maria Delores squinted, sure she could make out the Closed sign still in the window. There were no cars outside the shop and no sign of people inside. Still, she avoided the front and took a side street around to the back.

She stopped by the basement window and hesitated. A gentle push with her foot showed that the window still had not been fixed. She looked both ways, then slipped through the opening. She landed on her feet just below the window. It swung shut behind her, its dusty panes filtering out the sunlight.

Looking around in the dim light, she saw a sneaker on the concrete floor. She picked it up, her heart thumping. It was Julio's.

She crept cautiously across the floor, moving from crate to crate. A rustle from the corner made her jump. She held perfectly still until she saw a mouse scurry from beneath a crate. Then she sat down on a box before her legs gave way.

Where is Travis when I need him? she asked fiercely. Remembering the last time she was in the basement, she had a suspicion as to why Travis had been gone all afternoon. She crept forward again. When she reached the door beneath the stairs, she wasn't at all surprised to find it latched from the outside again.

She eased the latch open and pulled at the door. It swung open, and a form rushed out at her. She staggered backward as it hit her full force. She landed in a heap and shoved at the heavy weight pinning her down.

"Get off me!" she hissed. "Get off!!"

Travis scrambled to his feet. "Not again!"

"My words exactly," Maria Delores said furiously. "Do you always make a point of getting caught?"

Even in the shadows she didn't miss Travis's defensive look. "Good thing I left you a note," he said. He swiped his face with his hand, leaving a dark streak across his eyes.

"Note?"

"At the house."

When Maria still looked blank, he sighed. "Well, if you didn't find it, you're sure a good partner. Thanks for coming to the rescue again."

Maria Delores suddenly felt like she could handle just about anything. She glanced around. "Where is Julio?"

"Julio?" Travis looked horrified. "Don't tell me he's here too?"

"Then I won't," Maria Delores responded, getting to her feet. She looked toward the stairs. "But he is."

"Why?" Travis groaned.

"He came for his bag. He thinks he dropped it in the office when we found Kiwi," Maria explained.

"Let's go get him out of there," Travis whispered. "But keep quiet. Keith was *really* mad when he found me down here. I didn't think anybody could get that mad."

"Did he have a gun?" Maria Delores looked longingly at the broken window. "Maybe Julio isn't here after all."

"Yes, he had the gun, and he sure isn't afraid to use it," Travis said. "And if Keith thinks that 'jewel' is still in Julio's bag, then that bag is here. Along with the whole gang."

"They're a gang of . . ." Maria Delores's words stopped in her mouth. She stared at Travis. "How did you know?"

"You heard Angel. The word is out on the streets. I just asked around," Travis replied. "That snake guy really is bad news. When he finds out that Julio doesn't have the red jewel, who knows what he'll do to Julio. Come on!"

He started up the stairs before Maria Delores could tell him about the artist from Bogôtá. At the top, he motioned for her to be quiet. Then he opened the door a crack.

He slipped through without a sound. Quickly she followed. They were in the corridor beside the office. Travis went to his knees and crawled below the glass windows. The blinds were open. People moved about in the room, but their voices were muffled. When Travis waved Maria Delores on, she shook her head. She wanted to hear what was going on.

Turning the other direction, she crawled toward the showroom. She stopped a few feet from the door when she realized that it was cracked open. She heard Julio's voice.

"I told you I don't know where it is," Julio protested in a tired voice.

"Loosen his tongue a bit, Paulo," said an oily voice.

Maria slumped back against the wall. *Snake man!* A chill ran down her spine. Glancing up at the window, she saw the other shadow move toward the desk. A loud smack brought her upright again. She tensed. The man's hand came down again. *Smack!*

Chapter Fifteen
Captured!

The Galleria
Saturday, January 27ᵗʰ, 5:20 P.M.

Maria Delores was almost to her feet when a hand caught her from behind. Travis yanked her backwards. "He's hitting the desk," he whispered. "Julio didn't make a sound."

Maria let out her breath and settled back down, nerves on edge. She turned to look at Travis. As she did, she saw a movement in the dimly lit room. She grabbed Travis's shoulder, and he turned to look.

A head appeared around the corner of the showroom counter, and they were looking right into Keith's furious eyes. They froze as he began to inch toward them, moving noiselessly on his elbows. The total silence was more menacing than a sudden shout. Maria Delores shrank back against the wall, feeling along the edges for a weapon— any weapon.

About four feet from them, Keith stopped with a jerk. His unfocused eyes widened in shock. Then his body quivered and began to move backward. He clawed at the carpet but couldn't get a grip on anything that would stop that slow, backward slide.

Maria and Travis looked at each other. Maria shook her head in disbelief. Travis crawled after Keith. Maria followed hesitantly. She turned the corner in time to see Keith kicking and struggling in the grasp of the python.

"Snake!" she gasped. "Julio brought the snake!"

Travis stood up, grabbed a wooden bowl off the counter, and crashed it against Keith's head. He went limp.

As his playmate stopped struggling, the snake lost interest and slid away. Maria Delores bent over Keith. "He's still breathing," she said quietly.

The lights of the showroom flashed on. "How fortunate for you," a familiar voice said.

Maria Delores and Travis whirled around. Antonio stood behind them, smiling. "You saved us a nasty bit of work, kids," he said cheerfully.

"He's one of them," Travis said, pointing at the two men in the doorway of the office. "He's been . . ."

Events suddenly clicked in Maria Delores's mind. "No, Travis." She spoke quietly. "*He's* one of them."

Travis looked back at Antonio, then at the gun pointing straight at them. "Antonio?"

"Antonio, Carlos, Juan," Antonio said, still smiling. "I have many names. For now, Antonio will do."

A groan from the floor caused his smile to widen further. He waggled the gun at Keith, who had struggled to his hands and knees. "Meet Lieutenant Keith Taggert, one of Tampa Bay's finest."

Maria Delores and Travis stared at the man on the floor. "But he kept trying to run us off! He didn't want us around!"

"He's a policeman, dear," Antonio said. "He didn't want you in the middle of any action that might be dangerous. And as you can see, he was right. Now what am I to do with you?"

Keith groaned again and struggled to get up. One of the men in the doorway moved quickly. Before the groggy policeman could resist, his hands were firmly bound. As Antonio led Maria Delores and Travis into the office, Keith was yanked to his feet and shoved in behind them.

Julio watched them, eyes wide behind his glasses. He was in the chair by the desk, clutching his bag of stones.

"They're jewel thieves," he blurted out. "They want the jewel from Gran's lady."

"Ah, yes. Back to the jewel," Antonio began. "An unfortunate decision on the part of Mr. Valdes, who chose to take more than his share of our 'loot' as Julio calls it."

"He was part of your gang," Travis said in sudden understanding. "He helped sell the jewels!"

Maria Delores added, "And those the artist put on the paintings? Was that how he did it?"

"That's how he hid the ones he took from us," Antonio said. "It took a while to find out who, how, and where. Mauricio finally told us."

"The man in Bogôtá! You killed him!"

"Don't be silly, my dear. He was frightened, and his driving skills suffered, of course. The accident was just that—an accident. As you know, many accidents occur in the mountains."

"Like your parents?" Maria Delores asked, remembering the information on her tape recorder.

"Oh, no. My parents are alive and well, though I haven't seen them in some time. The accident in the Andes was just on my mind at the time I talked to you. Seemed like an interesting item for my little biography," he replied.

Travis stared. "You lead the gang of jewel thieves?"

"Sort of," Antonio smiled. "Meet my partner, Morton. Partners are quite useful you see, Travis. Especially if you work well together. And we do. My friends and I 'find' the jewels, and Morton here converts them to cash."

"And most of them came through this shop—until Valdes and his artist became greedy," Morton added. "There were just so many that they felt like a few would not be missed."

"And for a while, they got away with it," Antonio said. "Then they took the Albertine Ruby."

"One big job, and they were going to split. With our money!" Morton was irritated. "But they didn't get away with it."

"Neither will you," Travis said, looking at Keith. "If he knows, others know too."

"They won't be able to do anything about it until we're long gone," Antonio said sharply. "Paulo, take them downstairs. And put a chair against that door!"

Chapter Sixteen
An Unlikely Rescuer

The Galleria
Saturday, January 27th, 5:49 P.M.

Maria Delores followed Antonio down the stairs, wondering if she could trip Paulo. But Julio was right behind her, and Travis behind him. Someone would get hurt, and it might not be the bad guys.

Keith had recovered his senses. "Let the kids go," he told Antonio. "It'll go better for you if kids aren't mixed up in this."

Antonio laughed out loud. "Only if I get caught. And I don't plan to get caught. Since the kids don't have the jewel, that leaves only the dear, sweet grandmother. I'll have it within the hour."

Paulo shoved Keith into the small storeroom with Maria Delores, Travis, and Julio. The policeman hit a shelf and sank to his knees. The door slammed shut, and all light was cut off.

Keith groaned softly. Maria Delores asked, "Are you hurt?"

"Hurt? Why would I be hurt?" Keith snapped. "I tried to warn you kids off. You're not too quick on the uptake, are you?"

When Maria Delores didn't answer, Keith softened his tone. "Okay, I'll survive. A little bump isn't anything like being eaten by a snake. I hate snakes. Live snakes, dead snakes. Where is that thing anyway?"

"He wasn't trying to eat you. He's already been fed," Julio said in the darkness. "He was just trying to play."

"The gang didn't see him, did they?" Keith asked. "They don't know he's there?"

"No, but he's probably scared now," Julio answered. "He'll hide until things quiet down."

"Oh." Keith did not hide the disappointment in his voice.

"What are they going to do with us?" Maria Delores asked. "And what will happen to Gran?"

Keith avoided the first question. "Depends on whether she gives them the jewel or not."

"She doesn't have it," Maria Delores said in despair. "We gave it to Mr. Danbridge so he could evaluate it."

"Yes, she does," Julio said. "Or at least, she does now. She went to pick it up."

Travis groaned. "So he's going to get away."

"Maybe not," Keith said. "Can somebody pull the chain on that light?"

"No bulb in it," Travis said. "I should know."

"Why don't you use the ones on the shelf?" Maria Delores asked.

No one spoke for a minute.

"On the shelf?" Travis's voice sounded funny.

"Sure. That's where most people keep them," Maria Delores said. "Gran has hers where she can find them in a hurry."

"They're on the left," Keith said. He sounded amused.

She felt along the first shelf. As she touched some small boxes, one fell. There was a sharp pop as it hit the floor. "I found them," she said.

Touching the next box lightly, she pulled out a package of bulbs. "Here," she said, pushing one toward Travis.

He put out his hands and, after a moment, took the box from her. "Great," he said. "Now I'm supposed to put my finger in the socket?"

"There's a penlight in my shirt," Keith said. "It'll give enough light to find the socket."

Maria Delores held the penlight as Travis climbed on a stack of boxes to reach the hanging socket. He changed the bulb and pulled the chain. Light flooded the small room.

"Okay, kids," Keith said. "Get these ropes off me."

Travis found a sharp tool and sawed through the rope. Keith flexed his wrists and looked around. Travis watched him curiously.

"What are you looking at?" Keith finally asked.

"I want to see what you gather up to get us out. There's string here and chemicals . . ."

Keith gave him an incredulous look. "You've been watching too much television."

Travis toyed with the blade of the tool.

Keith watched him for a second. "Let me see that, kid," he said. Taking the tool, he inserted the thin blade into the crack of the door. He moved it up and down until the latch lifted.

"It's open," Maria Delores said.

Keith pushed against the door. It didn't open. He stepped back. "What kind of chair did they put against that door?"

Travis put his shoulder to the door. "We can all push."

"We're pushing against a chair, kid," Keith said impatiently. "The harder we push, the tighter we wedge the chair."

"We can try," Travis said stubbornly. "Mrs. O'Donnell is in trouble."

Keith sighed. "Okay, kid."

They made a running leap at the door, shoulders ready. The door swung open just before they reached it. Angel stepped aside just as Keith charged through. He tumbled full length on the floor with Travis on his back.

Travis scrambled to his feet.

"Angel!" Julio shouted.

"How did you find us?" Maria Delores asked, hugging the young girl.

"Don't mess the nails," she warned, hugging Maria Delores back. "If I couldn't follow you two, I'd be ashamed of myself."

"Where's Gran?" Maria Delores asked quickly. "She's in trouble!"

"She went to the house to see if you were there," Angel said. "Come on! The car's outside."

They charged up the stairs as Keith stuggled to his feet, groaning. "Stay out of this, kids!" he warned.

Chapter Seventeen
From Pest to Hero

Gran's House
Saturday, January 27th, 6:07 P.M.

As they raced through the showroom, Maria Delores saw the snake slither under a table. Julio slid after him.

The bell rang wildly as Angel yanked the door open and ran to her jeep. "Get in," she yelled, vaulting over the door. The jeep's engine roared as she threw the gear into reverse.

"Julio!" shouted Maria Delores. "Get in!"

Julio charged through the door and ran toward them, the snake bouncing around his shoulders. Maria Delores gritted her teeth and ignored the snake as she helped Travis pull her cousin into the jeep.

"What about Keith?" Travis said, looking back.

Maria Delores saw Keith stagger out the door and head for his car. "He has a transmitter in the car. The police will probably be there before us."

But they weren't.

The foyer door opened, but it wasn't Gran who let them in. It was Antonio. "Well, surprise," he said silkily. "Come on in."

Gran was seated in a chair. Maria Delores's heart caught in her throat. Never had Gran looked so ladylike. Her head was high, and she did not act afraid at all. At least she didn't until she saw the children.

"Now," said Antonio, moving behind Maria Delores. "Let's ask those questions again, Mrs. O'Donnell."

Gran looked at Maria Delores, Julio, Travis, and then at Angel. "All right," she said. "What you are looking for is in my purse. I picked it up today."

Snake man grabbed her purse and dumped the contents on the floor. The ruby flashed in the light. He grabbed it and held it up. "Forty carats," he said. "It'll go for over a million."

"A jewel thief, Antonio?" Gran said softly.

He bowed. "Indeed, ma'am."

"And Maria's message? The artist who died?"

"He and Mr. Valdes tried to cheat us," Antonio said, frowning. "Unfortunately, he involved you."

"I gather the loan of the paintings was not an act of generosity," Gran said. "He used me to protect the jewels on the velvet."

"When a buyer was found for one of the jewels, he replaced the painting with another," Antonio replied. "Your house was safe, above reproach. An ideal scheme, but one with a flaw."

"The jewel disappeared." Gran looked past Maria Delores, her eyes focusing on something in the hallway. Looking back at Antonio, she said carefully, "And you were out a bit of money."

Antonio's voice rose sharply. "More than a bit!"

Maria Delores did not see any movement beyond the living room, but she felt a difference in the air. Then from the darkness of the dining room came a series of agitated Spanish phrases, again in the voice she did not recognize.

"Mauricio? But he's dead!" Paulo moved away from Maria Delores. He backed toward the foyer.

"Impossible! It's a trick!" Antonio lunged toward the dining room. The unseen voice became louder and seemed to move toward him. Antonio dodged behind a wing chair, using it for cover.

The noise stopped.

The silence was more unnerving than the unseen voice. All eyes were fixed on the opening to the darkened room. No one heard the front door open; no one saw a stealthy movement in the foyer.

Antonio signaled his men to hold still. He rushed toward the dining room, ready to attack.

The voice from the foyer was cold and deadly. "Police! Freeze!"

"Get down, children," Gran commanded, sliding to the floor.

Antonio whirled and lifted his weapon. His eyes focused on the gun leveled on him and the tensed muscles of the policeman. He hesitated, then lowered his weapon.

Keith motioned toward the other men. "UP!"

Antonio and Paulo both raised their hands. Snake man hesitated, looking about wildly. The dining room held a talking dead man, and the foyer held a living, extremely angry policeman. He took a backward step and tripped over the snake. Hands grasping empty air, he crashed to the floor.

For a moment no one moved. Outside, sirens wailed and blue lights flashed through the windows as reinforcements arrived.

This time, it was really over.

"Come on out," Keith called to the stranger in the dining room.

Maria Delores began to smile. She heard the scrabble of claws on the wooden floor. Then a bedraggled Kiwi appeared in the light. He blinked and tilted his head unsteadily. "Wrap it up, Officer," he ordered.

"I should have known," Keith exploded. "That bird could have gotten us all killed!"

"Seems like we've heard that before," Gran said, smiling. "This time, though, Kiwi has gone from pest to hero."

Chapter Eighteen
Wrapping It Up

O'Donnell's Pet Shop
Saturday, February 3rd, 10:11 A.M.

Wrapping up the case was the easy part. Explaining it to others was not so easy. Kiwi ended up being the hero, as Gran had predicted. The story made an interesting beginning to the Gasparilla Festival, and Kiwi's photo on the front page brought curious buyers to the pet store.

"You don't look too happy, Maria Delores," Travis said as she pored over the story.

"I thought Keith was the bad guy, not Antonio. I guess I feel sort of . . ." she hesitated. "Stupid, I guess."

Gran put her good arm around Maria's shoulders. "You're not stupid, hon. We all judged people by what they said and didn't look any farther than that. Remember that old saying, 'You can't judge a book by its cover'?"

"Well, from now on, I'm looking a little harder," Maria Delores said.

"Me too," Travis agreed. "A good detective has to be a little sharper than we were. I thought Antonio was a cool guy."

"I didn't," said Julio.

When he was the center of attention, he hauled his cape around himself to hide his mouth. "I'm the one who sees all, who . . ." He stopped as they just looked at him. "Well anyway," he finished lamely. "He didn't like Kiwi."

"And anyone who doesn't like Kiwi is a bad person?" Gran asked.

When Julio nodded, she said, "I'm going to have to work on that one."

The next weekend, Keith came in with a girl about nineteen. She carried a knapsack over her shoulder like a student. When Kiwi saw her, he shrieked loudly. Fluttering wildly, he left his perch for her shoulder.

"This is Mauricio's sister, Katherine," Keith said. "She has come for Kiwi."

Maria Delores opened her mouth to protest. She closed it when she saw the way Kiwi was combing Katherine's dark hair with his beak. Katherine took the bird on her hand and talked to him softly in Spanish.

"The kids have been taking care of him," Keith told her. "Especially Julio."

"I want to thank you," Katherine told the children. "He is all I have left of my brother. Mauricio did many wrong things, but I loved him. He was my only brother. He didn't get along with my father. They fought often, and Mauricio became bitter. He fell in with the wrong people. I know that is no excuse for what he did, but I miss him so much."

She blinked and touched Kiwi's feathers. He immediately pecked her cheek gently. "Kiwi was his favorite. He kept him in the workroom with him. That's why Kiwi can speak English. Mauricio had the television on constantly to help improve his English. He wanted to come to America to work."

She looked puzzled when Travis laughed.

"That answers another question," Maria Delores explained. "Kiwi knows a lot about old television shows."

Katherine smiled. "Yes, my brother liked old police shows."

"But how did Kiwi get to America?" Travis asked.

"The men came to search the workroom, looking for the missing jewels. They argued with Mauricio, perhaps fought. Kiwi must have gotten out then, but I do not know how he got into that shipment to America," Katherine replied.

"I guess some mysteries will never be solved," Maria Delores said. "That's one. The other is how the first jewel got off the painting in the first place. That's what started this whole case, but that's the unanswered question."

"Was it sort of torn off?" Katherine asked.

When Maria Delores nodded, she laughed. "I can answer that one. Mr. Kiwi here got your case under way. Mauricio had trouble keeping him from taking the jewels and hiding them. He must be half-cousin to a magpie."

"I was right the first time!" Travis exclaimed. "Kiwi took it and hid it in Julio's room. Didn't you say you found it under the bed, Maria Delores?"

"Yes. I thought it was Julio's. I just put it in his bag," she answered.

"He started it all," Maria Delores said, ruffling Kiwi's feathers.

"And you're surprised?" Gran raised her eyebrows. "I'm not."

Julio hung on the counter and petted Kiwi. He said shakily, "We're going to miss Kiwi."

"I'll take good care of him," Katherine said. "I promise."

Julio petted Kiwi for the last time and let him go. The girl settled Kiwi's cage on the car seat beside her. Then she waved and was gone.

The shop seemed quiet. Too quiet. Gran looked at Julio and disappeared into the back. She came back out with the snake. "Julio, you did such a good job with Kiwi. Do you think you could take care of the snake for me?"

Julio looked up at her. His eyes began to sparkle. "You mean I can take it home? Really?"

"Really," Gran said.

Maria Delores wondered how Julio's mom would react to a snake in the house. Gran saw her thoughtful look and leaned over. "I already called," she whispered. "She's a good sport."

"Uh, huh," Maria Delores said, looking at the snake. "I'll bet she doesn't know what she's getting into."

Chapter Nineteen
The Parade

Tampa Bay
Saturday, February 17th, 11:14 A.M.

Two weeks later all five children found a place on the curb to watch the Children's Parade. Maria Delores beamed with pride when Gran's float inched its way down the street with the others.

"Hey," Mark said. "You guys did a great job!"

Corey agreed, then looked closer as the float passed. "Maria Delores," he said, "That kitten looks like . . ."

"What?" Maria Delores asked, eyes sparkling.

"Nah. Can't be."

Travis grinned and nudged Maria Delores, motioning for her to be quiet. He winked, and she understood. It was a secret.

A secret, she thought in amazement. *With Travis.* Would wonders never cease?

"Hey, hey!" Julio's excited shout interrupted her thoughts as he ran into the street with the other kids. The next float was shaped like a pirate ship. At the bow, a red-bearded pirate was scooping candy coins and fake jewels from a treasure chest. Roaring with laughter, he tossed them by the handfuls into the throng of screaming children.

Julio struggled back out of the crowd, hands full. "Hey, look what I got," he said happily.

Travis reappeared beside Maria Delores. "Look at that pirate," he said. "Doesn't he remind you of someone?"

Maria Delores took another look. "You know, there are hundreds of pirates in Tampa today," she said. "Just because he has a red beard doesn't mean a thing."

Travis relaxed. "Probably not."

As the float lumbered past, the man plunged his hands deep into the chest. Then he lifted his arm and threw a glittering mass over the heads of the crowd. His laugh rang out as golden candy rained around them. By the time they straightened up, the float was gone.

"Look what I got!" Mark held up a shiny plastic ring.

Maria Delores glanced at Julio, who had suddenly become quiet. He was holding a string of pearls.

"What is that, Julio?" she asked. "More stones for your bag?"

"No way," Julio said, thrusting the string of pearls at her. "No more stones for me!"

"Come on, Maria Delores," Travis called. "There are horses over here!"

Maria Delores pulled the string of pearls over her head and grabbed Julio's hand and started toward the boys. When she reached them, they made room for her. She pulled Julio in front of them so he could see the famous white stallions from Vienna.

"Wow! How do they do that?" he asked in wonder.

"Training," Travis yelled above the noise. "It takes years of training! Working together. Right, Maria Delores?"

"Right!" Maria Delores shouted back happily. Looking at Mark, she lowered her voice. "You'll have to change the Crimebusters' sign," she said.

He gave her a puzzled look. "Why?"

"Travis is not an associate," she said, looking Travis in the eyes. "He's a real Crimebuster now."

"All right!" Mark exclaimed. "You're in, Travis!"

"I'm in," Travis agreed.

Julio tugged on Maria Delores's hand. "Does that mean there's no associate?"

"Not exactly," Maria Delores replied, looking down at him.

As disappointment shadowed his face, she smiled. "You've just moved up to associate!"

"All right!" Julio yelled. "Can Albert come too?"

"Albert?" Maria Delores and the boys looked at each other. "Who's Albert?"

"My snake," Julio said proudly.

All four Crimebusters answered at once.

"No way! Absolutely no way!"